More Gore

from Cleveland

Thirteen Lovecrafted* Tales

By Craig A. Webb

Love-craft (luv-kraft) v. **-crafted -crafting**

To create, embellish, or imitate in style, spirit or content the horror writer Howard Phillips Lovercraft.

-Love'-craft-ism n. **-Love'craft-ist** or **Love'-kraft-er** n.

MORE GORE from CLEVELAND
Another 13 Lovecrafted Tales

Burning River Productions
1601 Cook Ave.
Cleveland, OH 44109-5632

Copyright © 2025 Craig A. Webb

Front and Back Cover photos: Korey Smerk, Owner/Creative @ Explored Perspective

Below Freezing photo: Photo by Jaunathan Gagnon on Unsplash

Author photo: Ria Terranova-Webb

All other photos: Craig A. Web

Front and Back Cover Design, Photo Manipulation and Book Layout: Ken Schworm

ISBN: 978-0-9968861-3-0

burningriver@msn.com

Dedications

My father; Robert Jay Webb
for scary stories told around the campfire

Special Thanks

Ken Schworm without whom this book would not exist
Laurie Kincer and The Skirball Writers Center
Susan Oelbracht and The Skyline Writers
Kristine Gill and The Willoughby Writers' Workshop

Howard Phillips Lovecraft (1890 – 1937) was a reclusive, little-known writer of fictional horror stories. Descending from a family beset by madness and suffering from fragile physical and emotional health, Lovecraft struggled to earn a living from his writing. He died in abject poverty of malnutrition and intestinal cancer.

However, admiring fellow writers published his tales of horrific elder gods, forbidden lore, and evil madness set in his beloved New England posthumously, giving birth to a unique genre of literary horror. Thus the dark, tortured genius of H.P. Lovecraft lives on—lurking in the shadows and inspiring these tales.

Contents

Salted Away

(Cleveland State University—Whiskey Island—Below Lake Erie)
First printed in the Ohio Writers' Association HOUSE OF SECRETS

Mindsight

Thingamajig

Tainted

Vanishing Point

The Bridge

Earwigs

(The Cleveland Clinic—The Unitarian Universalist Church)

List of Illustrations

Because I write "Local Horror," these are real places you may wish to visit, or not.

MORE GORE

from

CLEVELAND

Another 13 Lovecrafted* Tales

craig a. webb

*love-craft [luhv-kraft, -krahft] v. -crafted -crafting
To create, embellish, or imitate in style, spirit or
content the horror writer Howard Phillips Lovecraft.
-love-craftism n. -love-craftist or love-crafter n.

I was reminded of the stark utilitarian appearance of industrial Cleveland, a forgotten realm of muddy roadways, weedy fields and jumbled structures looking more like inhabited machinery than architecture.

Salted Away

"I've come from the salt mine," said the important-looking fellow led into my office by the department secretary.

"That's just great," I said. "Welcome to mine." I'd been struggling all week with the destruction caused by ISIS to the Assyrian World Heritage site of Nimrud and was in no mood for visitors. A modern political movement at war with ancient history made me want to strangle somebody.

"I'm from a real salt mine, Professor Stern. We've found something that might interest you." The idea something of value, to a classical archeologist like myself, could ever be found in Northeast Ohio was preposterous on the face of it. There was nothing remotely associated with my archaic period of expertise located closer than Mesoamerica (although I dabbled in excavations at the Serpent Mound in Southern Ohio for the benefit of my Cleveland State University students). Still, something of potential interest found under Lake Erie was sufficiently bizarre to merit attention.

Of course, I was aware salt is taken from man-made caverns far below Lake Erie. No doubt tours were available during my childhood years. Nowadays, the over-litigious nature of society renders such excursions impossible, although television crews are periodically allowed below for public relation purposes. You can Google some impressive subterranean vistas on the Internet.

* * *

Arriving at the mine headquarters, I was reminded of the starkly utilitarian appearance of industrial Cleveland, a forgotten realm of muddy roadways, weedy fields, and jumbled structures appearing more like inhabited machinery than architecture. It was a neighborhood solely constructed for trucks and trains, with miniature mountain ranges of raw materials drawn up from the depths below and piled several stories high all over the southern half of so-called Whiskey Island.

Richard Ivers, the superintendent of the facility and my uninvited visitor at Cleveland State, met me at the door. There were a number of safety procedures to review and a battery of liability waivers to sign before going below. A sternly worded contract of absolute secrecy gave me pause to consider the true nature of my visit.

"This is a three hundred million dollar operation," Superintendent Ivers said. 'We don't want trouble over anyone's academic hysteria…."

Suitably sworn and intrigued, I was led to the elevators. I envisioned some sort of gigantic, slanting tunnel into the underworld, but access consisted of only two vertical shafts. One for elevators delivering workers and machinery to and from the depths below, and the other for conveyer belts belching up salt from the mine.

* * *

Our descent was 1,800 feet of semi-dark clattering, with rough stone walls rising slowly past dirty, screen-reinforced windows. Ivers and I wore hard hats and reflective vests and each carried a large battery-powered hand lamp, plastic bottle of water, and emergency cylinder of oxygen said to last one hour.

"If they can't dig you out by then, you're probably dead already," explained my stoic companion. This was the first time Ivers brought up the prospect of mortality. An immediate vision of being crushed under tons of salt, somewhat tempered my former enthusiasm.

At the bottom of the shaft, we stepped out into a small island of light spilling from the elevator cabin surrounded by a dry, surprisingly warm realm of absolute darkness.

"The salt sucks all the moisture out of the air and radiates a certain amount of chemical heat," Ivers said.

"Why so dark?" I asked, expecting at least minimal illumination in the vast system of passageways.

"There's over four square miles of cavern down here Professor. It's too expensive to light anywhere we're not actually working."

We boarded a modified electric golf cart carrying a smattering of tools and started down the mammoth corridors only partially illuminated by our headlights. I felt like we were traversing nocturnal desert ruins with 50-foot halite walls of rock salt on every side and sand-like layers of loose salt under our tires. Only when using my hand lamp could I glimpse the continuous overhead ceiling of rocky, machine-carved salt forming our oppressive sky.

The corridor was cross-cut at regular intervals by similar corridors going in perpendicular directions. My hand lamp revealed these were themselves intersected by numerous corridors parallel to our own. The entire cavern system must be a gargantuan grid-work of mined passageways interspersed by solid floor-to-ceiling blocks of salt crystal—a hidden cathedral of darkness beneath my everyday world. I imagined Hades himself would find it spacious.

"Why leave so much salt behind?" I said.

"To hold the roof up. There's at least 1,500 feet of solid rock and clay above the salt layer and millions of tons of Lake Erie water above that. At least a quarter of the entire area must remain as salt pillars. The spacing is critical to bear the load."

"Has the lake ever broken through?"

"Not here. There was a collapse under Lake Michigan. They blamed it on an earthquake, but the seismic shocks may have been caused by catastrophic roof failure."

"Would we all drown?" I asked, now imagining a second mode of personal annihilation.

"Not unless we were directly under the breach," Ivers said. "It would take days to fill the entire cavern. You're not going to drown, Professor. You're more likely to get lost down here in the dark and die of dehydration." That completed a trifecta of lethality I'd never considered previously. *Who calls archeology boring?* I thought. *When I'm faced with so many lethal dangers by simply leaving the office?*

* * *

Deeper into the mine, we began to run into traffic. Enormous front-end loaders roared down corridors bringing newly crushed salt to the conveyors. They were lowered into the mine in pieces and assembled below. Anything that broke down and could not be repaired on-site was left behind. Elephantine graveyards of discarded machinery sat rusting away in played-out sections of this vast salt maze. *Someday,* I imagined. *Archeologists will consider this forgotten horde a gold mine of ancient technology.*

After an hour of driving, we arrived at a corridor blocked off by drilling equipment and caution tape. Ivers got out and cleared a passage for us to drive through.

"Remember Professor Stern," he said. "Nobody hears anything about what you find here except me—absolutely nobody." By this time I had imagined a thousand improbable discoveries that might lay ahead, from lost anchors to a marooned time machine. Now, after his morbid disclosures and reenforced warning, I pictured mass graves of miners or sailors from some forgotten past.

The corridor continued for about 300 feet until we came to a partially excavated dead end. Ivers parked our cart and shut off the headlights leaving us submerged in utter darkness. He searched about with his hand lamp until finding a gas-powered generator atop a left over ridge of loose salt. Starting it, the hollowed-out area beyond the salt ridge became illuminated by work lights. A palpable feeling of awe and dread swept over me as I wondered what lay beyond. Ivers laughed from atop the ridge at my obvious hesitation.

"Come on Professor Samuel Stern," he said. "History

isn't going to write itself." Suitably chastised, I clawed my way up to where he stood.

At first, I saw nothing but a jumble of rock salt boulders strewn against the irregular corridor end. If there was some fossil or archeological pattern I was supposed to find, it was not immediately apparent.

I looked toward Ivers for clarification, but he simply indicated I should go closer. As I struggled down the other side of the tumbled salt ridge, a strange anomaly came into view. Amid all those jagged, machine-scarred surfaces, an area of less crystalline whiteness embedded in the wall came into focus. It rose three to four feet from the floor and appeared to be an exposed segment of a curve, like a portion of a column or the edge of a raised dais.

I knelt beside it at an angle not blocking the work lights and rubbed the exposed surface with my hand. The distinctive feel, so reminiscent of other antiquities I've encountered, was unmistakable.

"This isn't salt, is it?" I said.

"Marble," he answered. "I chipped off a piece to test it. But it's not uncommon to hit upon impurities down here, outcroppings of stone, even fossilized coral reefs. This salt was deposited at the bottom of an inland sea."

"It seems man-made—carved and smoothed by someone," I said.

Now Richard Ivers paused. He stared up toward the rugged ceiling for a moment, exhaled a long sigh, and then walked down the salt ridge toward me.

"That's what I thought," he said. "I was hoping to be wrong." He sat down beside me and placed his hand on the smooth surface. "Are you sure this can't be some kind of natural formation? I mean, who could have done this? Please don't tell me I've found Atlantis in the middle of Lake Erie."

"I honestly do not know," I said. "How old are these salt strata?"

"Fifty million years, more or less."

"Fifty million! Then nobody did this. Nobody human anyway."

"Damn it!" he swore, jumping up and heaving a chunk of salt explosively against the corridor wall. "You said it was man-made. Try to make sense, will you!"

"Well," I sputtered. "I mean, it looks manufactured… or carved, at least. That's not to say humans had to make it. Evolutionary science would say there were no humans 50 million years ago, especially in North America. There were other creatures, of course, dinosaurs and so on, but we've never discovered any other creature known to create or modify objects like humans do."

"So Professor Samuel Stern," he bellowed. "This thing—this thing right in front of our eyes can't exist? You and I are imagining the whole God-damn thing?"

"Hold on," I said. "There must be some explanation. For instance, look at these salt walls around us." We both turned our hand lamps on the surrounding walls. "See these horizontal striations. See the layers and the slightly different colors of the salt."

"Yes, We know all about that," he said. "Laid down over millions of years as conditions changed year by year until the ancient sea dried up. The whole salt deposit looks like this."

"Not quite true. Look at the salt wall over our, um…
artifact, shall we say. Notice how the horizontal striations
are gone. The colors are all mixed up, possibly even verti-
cally oriented. Someone, conceivably much later in time,
could have excavated a hole in the salt, placed the artifact
here, and covered it up again."

"Yes!" he said. "I can see that. The…artifact could be
from any time after the sea dried up, lost or hidden in the
lake, then forgotten. But who would do that?"

"We still don't know," I said. "But it's a workable hy-
pothesis. We'll remove the salt around it and examine more
closely. There may be markings to provide the answer."

Ivers agreed to assign a trusted group of miners to the
project. They would have to work slowly, as heavy machinery and explosives were inappropriate. There would need
to be supportive scaffolding erected around the artifact
to stabilize the ceiling, if indeed it had been previously
excavated.

I calculated the probable diameter of the artifact to be
20 feet if it were, in fact, circular, and Ivers estimated the
work would be completed in three days. We both left the
mine with high expectations of momentous discovery. All
former shadows of doom completely fled my mind under
the white hot light of true discovery.

* * *

The next time I visited the location, I found the work
of Ivers' men impressive, but the artifact itself far less

so. The barrier ridge of salt rubble was gone, and our workspace was well-lit and spacious. The floor-to-ceiling scaffolding looked sturdy as it ringed the exposed artifact at a respectful distance allowing unimpeded access from any angle.

The artifact, however, appeared disappointingly utilitarian—like a huge vertical drainpipe with a cap. The top rose just over three feet above the salt floor, presenting a slightly domed circular appearance. The entire thing was approximately twenty feet in diameter, as expected, and the depth to which it might extend below the cavern floor was unknown.

"Not much to it," said Ivers as we stood together assessing the situation.

"Could it be part of the municipal water system?" I asked. "It looks vaguely industrial."

"This area of the mine is way out beyond the intake crib for Cleveland's water supply."

"Maybe a piling for some never-completed pier or lighthouse?"

"Not according to anything we can find in city records," Ivers said. "Even in the 1800s they would have built a cofferdam, pumped the water out, and poured concrete. Nobody uses carved marble unless it's meant to be seen."

I walked down to run my hands over the newly exposed top and found the surface rough and gritty. This was not the smooth marble of the original surface.

"This still feels like salt."

"It is. The guys were using power tools and didn't want to scar it by cutting in too close."

"Then let's get some hand tools and really get a look at it!" I shouted.

* * *

Our handwork made all the difference. The sides still presented a smooth curve of polished stone, but the top rim was heavily carved with shallow, inset markings visible from both side and top. The domed cap proved even more elaborate, with two dramatic arched ridges perforated at regular intervals and meeting in the center to divide the circular whole into four distinct segments.

Inside these segments, a rich pictographic style took over, presenting a possible storyline or sequence of events that thrilled us with every scrape of chisel and sweep of cleaning brush. Ivers had everything photographed, and I made detailed drawings and rubbings of every inch of carved surface. I imagined the happy years I would spend researching their origin and meaning.

The rim markings were clearly some unknown form of writing composed entirely of intersecting circles, dots, and spirals. Better still, these seemed to repeat the same complex phrase or word multiple times, so its entirety could be perceived at any angle from top or side. Whatever this word or phrase meant, it was obviously important, although, of course, absolutely meaningless to us.

The pictographs were even more cryptic, consisting of three types of symbols superimposed upon wavy backgrounds of deeper incisions. The three symbols were small ovals with four declining curved lines (possibly representing individuals but appearing more jellyfish or mushroom than human), rectangular boxes of various sizes (possibly dwellings), and a cloud-like mass or growth appearing to increase in size from segment to segment (to which we could assign no meaning whatsoever).

In the two opposing crescent segments, the oval figures and box combinations increased in number and complexity within close association to the cloud. The two smaller triangular segments showed the ovals and boxes decreasing with the cloud's expansion.

* * *

Much later, as I went over the day's momentous findings in my office, a feature of the rim markings struck me. The repetitive dots, while making up a small portion of the whole, were always displayed in varied groupings of five. This feature triggered an ominous flash of recall. Somewhere I had seen or read about this repetition of dots before…with some context of fear or menace.

I ran computer checks on all known archaic writing systems and found nothing. I scrolled through my pictures of Nimrud, thinking there was some ISIS connection or even some reference to the ancient cities of Ur, Babylon, or Assyria. Finally, I tried a broad Google search, which kicked up an obscure reference to a deceased author of fantastically grotesque fiction, a Mr. H. P. Lovecraft.

"Yes," I thought. *"I used to read this guy in high school."* I remembered some absurd tale of Antarctic exploration and frozen plant-beings still lurking in my subconscious

containing this five-dot symbolism. I laughed aloud at the unlikely coincidence, deciding to reread this fanciful story when I found the time.

* * *

I was called back to the mine two days later without making any progress in identifying the source of the artifact. Superintendent Ivers introduced me to a young intern named Henry Danforth working with his engineering department. Henry had designed the scaffolding surrounding our artifact and, during his daily inspections, discovered something important.

"This will knock your socks off," Henry said.

Danforth, Ivers, and I descended into the mine, drove to the well-guarded corridor, and approached the artifact. The young man took a small rock hammer and asked Ivers to kill the noisy generator powering the work lights. In the resultant silence, illuminated by our hand lamps, we watched him tap the side of the artifact. It gave forth a solid sound, which was repeated as he tapped the upper rim—being careful to avoid marring the carved markings. Then he carefully tapped the top of the artifact on one of the arched ridges. The sound produced was startlingly different. As Ivers and I drew closer, Henry tried several other top locations to similar effect.

"It's definitely hollow," he said. "And I think I know how to open it up." In retrospect, we should have postponed this irreversible step—but I am an archeologist. We always brave the desert or the jungle. We always open the tomb. The unknown is just that addictive.

* * *

While Ivers and I were fascinated by exotic markings, Danforth had focused on the artifact's construction. He probed everywhere he guessed the salt coating might hide a seam or joint.

Based on his careful observations, he felt the pictographic top rotated out of the thicker, marking-covered rim. He thought the key was the arched ridges and the small stone wedges he discovered locking this cover plate where each ridge met the rim.

We quickly organized the necessary equipment to test his theory. Five hours later, we had a small mobile crane ready to hoist the lid by chains hooked into the perforations on the two arched ridges (which now seemed obviously positioned for just such a purpose). Henry worked at the supposed wedges with his pocketknife, a pair of locking pliers, and a can of WD-40 spray lubricant.

Amazingly the four wedges came out with minimal effort. Danforth signaled for the crane operator to exert a small amount of lift and began knocking sequentially on the four ridge endings with a rubber, auto-body mallet. When minor rotation was detected, Ivers assigned three more workers with mallets to assist in the careful hammering at all four ridge ends.

Slowly and with generous amounts of lubricant, the top plate rotated free. Danforth gave the signal to raise it up. A moment later, we were all hit with the most terrible, wretched stench anyone had ever experienced.

Our entire workforce retreated down the mine corridor as far as the caution tape barrier, with a good deal of vomiting along the way. Electric ventilator fans were brought in to help circulate air, but fifty steps down the corridor was the most anyone could withstand. Ivers felt there was danger of an explosion or possible health risk. It would take days to have the air tested. He decided we'd have to shut down the investigation until then, but his young engineer was too impatient for such bureaucratic temerity.

"Look," Danforth said, flicking on his plastic cigarette lighter. "Not flammable, see. The engine of the crane would have set it off by now if it were. I vote we see what's in that damn thing today!"

"I could fire you for that," Ivers yelled. "Who said you get a vote? What if it's poison gas?"

"Nobody's skin is burning. Nobody passed out," Danforth argued. "Sure, it smells like holy hell, and the air is hard to breathe, but that's why we carry oxygen down here."

"All right, smart guy," Ivers finally said. "You can take a look—if you can get anyone else to go with you."

The rest of the crew stepped away from the young, firebrand engineer with screwed-up faces of revulsion and distrust. It looked like the Superintendent would have his delay until I raised my hand. I feared we might have already triggered some primeval burial curse or even worse—so why worry about an ancient stink bomb?

Danforth and I improvised gas masks by stuffing our noses with Kleenex and using our oxygen tanks to avoid breathing the putrid air. It wasn't perfect, but it cut the smell enough to let oxygen and curiosity energize our work.

At the rim of the artifact, we shone our hand lamps down into a dozen feet of empty stone cylinder and onto a glistening gelatinous pool of inky-black goo.

"Damn," the young man said. "What the hell died in here?"

"Only one way to find out," I said, and we began to improvise the means to gather a specimen. Carrying only one hour of oxygen each, a degree of caution had to be forfeited. The pictographic lid was lowered to the floor, and the chains dangling from the crane's cable were fashioned into a sling. Only Danforth knew how to operate the crane. Therefore, I reluctantly volunteered to enter the ominous stone vessel.

Carrying an emptied glass bottle and screw-on lid from some miner's lunch, I arranged myself on the chain sling and was lowered into the cylinder. Since there were only two of us, and Danforth had to stay with the crane that made excessive engine noise, we devised a system of hand lamp signals in the darkened workspace.

The darkness of the cavern above and the glistening pool of blackness below made for a nervous descent. I had no desire to touch the inky substance with so much as my shoe. It took a delicate maneuver getting close enough to scoop some into the jar. Even more so when I discovered the pool's surface was congealed into a rubbery pulp. I had to utilize my own pocket knife to slice out a viscous sliver and skewer it into the jar.

In doing so, my hand lamp slipped from my lap and

landed on the gelatinous black surface. It seemed to trigger a slow, sinuous ripple moving out to the surrounding cylinder edge in a disturbingly animate manner. I snatched the lamp from the opaque surface, terrified of losing my means to signal for an escape, and flashed it desperately above for Danforth's attention. Mercifully, he responded and raised me up above the glistening, dark mass, as it continued a languorous undulation seemingly quite out of proportion to the disturbance I'd created.

* * *

Back at Cleveland State, I commandeered a biology lab and prepared a smear of my carbonaceous specimen on a microscope slide. Under high magnification I observed the substance seemed to be an agglutination of iridescent black bubbles. So small a sample did not give out the unbearable stench of the entire mass but was still distastefully pungent.

I utilized a drop of sterile liquid to prepare the slide and found it absorbed into the substance quickly. This lubrication appeared to create cellular movement as the bubbles expanded before my eyes. Had I not been positive the specimen had endured ages of internment, I would have sworn it was still alive.

Obviously, as an archeologist, I was far outside my field of training. I would ask a biology professor or a petroleum engineer to examine this unknown substance in the morning. I sterilized the slide with some alcohol and prepared to lock up.

Turning to collect my bottle, I was startled to see the specimen, initially the size and shape of a large garden slug, now completely filling the sealed container and churning inside like a liquid swarm of coal-black maggots. Afraid to touch it, I watched the bottle burst and gelatinous ooze spread over the metal lab countertop.

It was only then I remembered the ultimate horror revealed in that obscure Lovecraft fiction. *"The thing that should not be"* that bubbled up from some volcanic abyss to swallow and absorb all life before it—the fetid, murderous effervescence he called a Shoggoth.

I poured the bottle of alcohol over the expanding black slime. When it caused no effect, I ignited the volatile fluid with a Bunsen burner. Still, the flaming, viscous jelly grew and cast out slithering appendages of ooze as if searching to gain the floor.

Fearing I made matters worse by introducing a fire hazard, I grabbed the large CO2 fire extinguisher from the lab wall and smothered the protoplasmic abomination with clouds of freezing vapor. The flames extinguished, and better yet, the creeping black mass retracted and diminished into an inert blob. I emptied the extinguisher on the damned thing, scooped it into a lockable metal container with the help of a lab tray, and stashed it in a cryogenic freezer where I prayed it would remain harmless barring a lengthy power failure.

Afterward I was so overcome with fear and adrenaline that I slumped to the floor and lay there panting like a winded sprinter until my heart slowed to a bearable rhythm. Then I remembered the salt mine, where the cylinder was still open and the great bulk of the creature lay totally unfettered.

I shot to my feet, almost fainting again from the shocking realization of the danger I helped release. Immediately I called Superintendent Ivers at the mine headquarters to warn against approaching the artifact for any reason except to replace the lid.

"I'm way ahead of you," he said. "We're going to dig this putrid thing up and haul it out of the mine entirely. Danforth is down inside now probing how deep that black shit goes...."

* * *

By the time I raced to the worksite, the worst had already happened, or so we thought. Poor Henry Danforth, harnessed safely to a wooden platform attached to the crane's cables, had been carefully lowered into the mouth of the cylinder carrying a ten-foot length of steel rebar.

The acrid stench of the black mass had dissipated sufficiently for Henry and the rest of the workers to breathe through simple painting masks, although the result was still exceedingly unpleasant. As his crew mates watched from the rim, Danforth began to thrust his steel rod into the placid, opaque mass of goo. What happened next was still under debate.

"It sucked him down!" one worker said. "Took the rebar and all."

"No," said another. "It came up and grabbed him. A big black claw of liquid fingers came up from all around the edges and closed over him like a fist!"

Whatever happened, it was clear Danforth had not fallen—since he was tightly harnessed as per OSHA regulations about the waist and shoulders. His complete disappearance suggested (however horribly) he was torn apart in the process. One terrifying scream was uttered, and then nothing except the agitated sloshing of the black slime pool. Sending a second man down to try a rescue was out of the question.

Huddling with the grief-stricken mine superintendent and workers, I described my experience in the lab and my admittedly outlandish appraisal of our danger. Their reaction was both alarmed and incredulous.

"You're talking science fiction!" Ivers shouted. "I've lost a good man to something, but not some made-up monster from a ghost story."

I explained that the "fictional" sometimes manifests in real life. If something is conceivable by man (Lovecraft certainly pulled this creature from his own troubled psyche), then it may actually exist. Before getting into examples of Jules Verne's Nautilus and Star Trek's communicators, the creature proved my point.

Danforth's platform, still dangling below, abruptly took a tremendous hit and splintered apart. Something began pulling on the chains with such force that the tip of the crane's boom slammed down to the rim of the stone cylinder lifting the back tires of the crane off the floor—displaying the awesome power and weight of whatever was climbing up.

To witness such a thing is to lose forever that part of

your rational mind defining what is possible and what is not. What bubbled, crawled, or slithered out of that damned hole was glistening black madness. To say we were all *"like deer in the headlights"* is to imagine the laws of time and physics were still in play and not decimated by the horror oozing up over the cylinder, crane, and scaffolding like a slow-motion eruption of iridescent evil.

We staggered backward, unable to take our eyes off the abomination's advance. And it had eyes on us too—hundreds of them extending out on pustule stalks of ooze to peer at us with greenish glowing intensity. Mouths it had also, opening up in disgusting volume and all uttering forth the single fatal scream copied from poor Danforth. Chaos and unstoppable doom had broken loose, and we would all soon be trapped deep underground with it…in the dark.

Helpless and hopeless as we were, the Earth itself and the unknown ancients who buried the artifact came to our rescue. This squirming, slithering fountain of living glop had a weakness, a weakness that lay all around us. Wherever it flopped onto the loose salt of the cavern floor, a sizzling steam arose. Salt dissolved the creature at the slightest touch like a common garden slug, and except for the stone cylinder, crane and scaffolding—salt was all there was in these caverns.

Everything that bubbled forth dissolved on contact with the floor, walls, or ceiling. The scream—the only voice the creature possessed, echoed throughout the cavern as it gained some primitive understanding of its captive fate.

Slowly it began to diminish, dissolving into a putrid, oily stain and retreating to its sanctuary of stone. We began using shovels and even our hands to throw more salt upon it. Ivers ordered men with front-end loaders to bury the damn thing in a white crystalline avalanche.

Eventually, I convinced him against totally destroying the creature. Who knows what could be learned from such an implausible beast? Instead, we resealed the artifact, buried it under loose salt, and closed off that corridor. I had a frozen specimen at the university and all the photographs and drawings needed to document this astounding encounter.

I began this adventure enraged over a present day attack on ancient history. Now I understand that ancient history could return that aggression on the present. If a Shoggoth still survived, what about its original captors? Did they intend to punish it or preserve it for some future purpose? And how, in God's name, did Lovecraft guess at their existence? Of all the questions remaining, the unknown phrase on the cylinder rim still haunts me nightly. Perhaps I will understand its message someday. But for now, I translate it as—*Danger: Do not open!*

Crawford and I moved in tandem—eventually rooming together at the same university, attending medical school, doing our residencies at the Cleveland Clinic and settling nearby in a brick double on Random Road in Little Italy.

Mindsight

Crawford had always been an odd duck. In medical school his superior intellect always seemed focused elsewhere. Perhaps he did know more than our instructors, but it was never wise to say so. The predictable result, despite his academic record, was finding himself marooned with the likes of me, a lackluster scholar at best, in the imaging departments of the Cleveland Clinic—primarily because his bedside manner was considered "both aloof and morbid."

I was content working in radiology, MRI's and CAT scans, but Crawford seemed unsatisfied. Of course he was competent, and occasionally brilliant, but that was never sufficient for him.

"Oh, my God," he groaned. "Is this really the best we can do?"

"Problem?" I asked. "Looks like a clear enough image to me."

"Does it, Minh? What do you conclude from this mere shadow of reality?"

"A medium size mass in the lower left lung? We should recommend a biopsy and check it out—good chance it's a tumor."

"Good chance you say? Better than a fifty-fifty? Of

course it's a fucking tumor! Any idiot knows that. Mister What's-his-name is a smoker, cancer runs in his family, he's a dead man walking. But how does that tumor feel, Minh? And why does it only manifest at sixty-five? Why the left lung, not the right?"

"Uhm . . . how does Mr. Greenspan feel, or the tumor itself?"

"Both, you moron!" he shouted, tossing the image at me and stalking out.

* * *

Perhaps his behavior seems abusive. I'm told others found it intolerable and was often questioned about my own rather submissive attitude toward such displays.

The truth is Crawford Townsend was my best friend since childhood. I can barely remember a day he was not thrashing around somewhere in the outer periphery of my life. Always slightly older, slightly taller and whiter by a mile, but haunted by a certain dissatisfaction that darkened his otherwise all-American countenance. He was "Goth" by nature before it became a cultural fashion.

Both our families were well-to-do but emotionally distant. We both had other siblings who were bright, amicable and photogenic, providing a smokescreen of domestic bliss behind which Crawford and I were left free to roam wild and fester. You might say we "raised" each other.

"What are you so damn happy about?" he used to grumble.

"Oh nothing," I would gush with amusement knowing

it drove him to distraction. "I guess I'm just a glass-half-full kind of guy."

"Your glass has been filled to overflowing since kindergarten," he would snarl. "I wish you would finally drown yourself in it!"

"Then who would cheer you up, when you're feeling blue?" I would twinkle.

"Nobody!" he'd roar, "And that would make me very cheerful indeed."

As others in our generation ran with the pack, formed cliques and joined teams, Crawford and I moved in tandem—eventually rooming together at the same university, attending medical school, doing our residencies at the Clinic and settling nearby in a brick double on Random Road in Little Italy. I took the top suite with abundant light, unobstructed views all the way to Lake Erie and a cozy balcony to share with acquaintances and lovers. Crawford lived below, behind locked doors and black-out curtains where he had exclusive access to the basement for "experimentation."

I should mention neither of us were boy scouts. Much of what went on at that time and location was tolerated, but not strictly legal. For instance, we both preferred male company, although Crawford may have been exclusive (if infrequently), with me. We both enjoyed pharmaceuticals (medical and otherwise), although "employed" might better describe Crawford's usage. In those times of AIDS, addiction & moral decay, our medical training kept most consequences at bay. That ended with the covid pandemic.

* * *

Everyone thinks they know what it was like in hospitals during the worst of the pandemic. The media covered it extensively (from a safe distance). But it was much, much worse. We lived with death constantly. We ate with it, we slept with it, we took it home with us and brought it back in the morning. I was an emotional wreck. But Crawford was, I hesitate to say . . . somewhat invigorated.

In the evening we commiserated outside together on my balcony, because neither apartment was air conditioned and total, social isolation became intolerable. After twelve to twenty hour shifts (there was no hiding behind our X-rays now, everyone was in the trenches), I looked like a medieval penitent: hollow-eyed, exhausted, reduced to skin and bones. Crawford paradoxically seemed ever stronger, resembling a dark Adonis, like Jim Morrison with shorter hair clipped by surgical scissors.

"Minh," he said, as we sweltered together in the twilight glimmer of one onrushing night. "I've been working on something. Would you like to see?"

"Will it hurt or cause a rash like those Kama Sutra poses?" I said.

"Funny you should ask. Remember me wanting to feel Mr. Greenspan's tumor?"

"Ah . . . vaguely."

"Well now I can," he said and smiled.

"He's been dead for over a year."

"But not forgotten. Come along downstairs and I'll demonstrate."

* * *

I didn't enjoy visiting Crawford's apartment. The sparse, leather and chrome furniture seemed cold even in this summer heat. He favored a minimalist style, two-tone color scheme and absolutely nothing on his walls. He thought it artistic. I called it "vampire modern." It resembled the waiting room of a mortuary, minus artificial plants.

I idled around his virtually sterile kitchen waiting for a preliminary cocktail and some sly, outrageous excuse to break out the latex, blindfold and handcuffs, but he simply began to unlock his elaborate security on the door to the basement steps.

"Oh, you meant all the way downstairs," I murmured.

"Yes Minh," he said dryly. "I'm sorry if you had lurid entertainment in mind—perhaps another evening. Tonight will be about science and discovery, although restraints will be involved. Does that help whet your appetite?"

It didn't, but demotion from playmate to lab rat was not abnormal. I helped set up his "laboratory" on moving in and sometimes played Igor to his Baron Frankenstein.

The basement was old, unfinished brick and concrete, but he'd spent a good deal of time and money insuring it was clean, dry and furnished with plumbing and electricity. There was an array of equipment hung around the walls, rolling work and examination tables and even a walk-in cooler for storage of perishable specimens. Crawford pointed to an elaborate wooden chair centered in the space and said, "Assume the position." I sat down prepared for anything but what actually happened. "You'll recall my comments about feeling not only Mr. Greenspan's pain, but also the perception of the tumor itself. No doubt you found that . . . unreasonable."

"No shit—but I know you were pissed at me during that conversation."

"Not at you Minh, but with you. Because you failed to see the value of physicians actually experiencing the discomfort, shall we say, of the patient directly."

"You want to feel their pain, like with a broken leg or burst appendix? What doctor, in his right mind, would want to do that?"

"Someone trained in human anatomy," Crawford said, circling me like the prosecuting attorney at a murder trial. "Someone longing to know the exact location, severity and condition of the afflicted. Would that not assist successful treatment?"

"Who would agree to catch cancer in order to cure it?" I snapped back.

"Who indeed?" He sneered, suddenly pinioning my wrists, ankles, neck and chest to the chair by triggering a series of devious, spring-loaded restraints. "Now let us test the limits of your professional empathy, shall we Minh?"

"Are you going to torture me?" I yelled.

"Calm yourself fool. Have I ever inflicted anything on you that I haven't suffered? The restraints are for your protection. In just a moment, I will torture myself."

I didn't believe that, but couldn't dismiss it outright. Crawford could be prodigiously perverse on occasion—and this felt like just such an opportunity. He produced a light, wiry apparatus and fitted it on my head with special attention to my temples and forehead.

"How many volts am I in for?" I asked nervously.

"Never fear, you're not plugged in," he said. "This cranial lattice only uses watch batteries to stimulate both brain lobes and your pituitary gland—the so-called 'third eye' you South Asian types are so intent on opening."

"Buddhists don't use shock therapy. That sounds more Southern Baptist to me."

"You'll experience nothing but a slight vibration and a bit of tinnitus, I promise. Now," he said, pulling up a second chair and sitting down six to eight feet away. "I want you to calm your mind and match your breathing to mine . . . in, out, in, out, in, out. You may close your eyes if you like." I did not like and watched him intently, waiting for his steel-gray eyes to betray a next move. But they did not.

Instead he produced a hidden pen knife and plunged it viciously into the meat of his left hand. I screamed in pain, looking to my own pinioned hand for the extent of the damage. But my hand was untouched, although as painful as before! Crawford calmly withdrew the knife, raised his hand and showed me the bloody result.

"Need to examine my handiwork, or can you already feel the diagnosis?"

"It's a clean flesh wound," I said. "You missed all the bones and arteries . . . but you are still an absolute lunatic!"

"And a skillful surgeon," he said, getting up and walking to his workbench behind me. "If you'll excuse me I must attend to this bleeding." My own hand still hurt and even felt as if it were being sanitized and bandaged invisibly. Suddenly I felt as if my testicles were being painfully squeezed.

"What the hell Crawford!" I shouted. "You've proved your point!"

"Sorry," he chuckled. "I had to test if your first reaction had anything to do with anticipating my knife thrust—my bad."

"Well congratulations, it certainly works—seen or unseen. But beyond an initial diagnosis who would use such a device? My hand is still throbbing."

"And will as long as mine does—if you keep wearing the brain lattice. A serious design limitation I'm afraid. I've tried using it in the hospital hidden under my personal protection gear, but with so many sick and dying around me I could not function properly under it's multiple effects."

"That makes sense, but it's not a total failure. You could still use it one-on-one for immediate diagnosis and then take it off—maybe even automate it to show up on an electronic screen like some kind of physical sensation X-ray."

"I think it requires a living receiver to feel the connection," Crawford mused, coming back around before me. "But there's something else we must investigate," he said, circling the other chair ominously. "Minh, I have watched people die."

For a moment I did not catch his meaning. I simply felt compassion for my fellow caregiver. "We all have," I said. "It's terrible, but the trauma we feel comes from the sheer amount of death we're seeing lately."

"Oh boo-fucking-hoo," he taunted. "You feel so inadequate. There's blood on your hands. Think I give a damn? I've watched them die wearing this brain lattice."

I sensed a dangerous mood rising over Crawford. As his captive audience, I tried to dampen that down immediately.

"But you didn't die along with them—so that's promising. What did you see?"

"I don't know, I'm not sure," he whined. "There were so many emotions and sensations of sickness coming at me all at once. And nobody else was wearing a brain lattice, so my perception was murky at best."

"You talk about watching, about vision. You said the lattice transmits feelings."

"It transmits and receives feelings—which create mental images," he confessed. "Did you not see my knife stab into your own flesh, at least momentarily?" I realized I had, and possibly the mental image generated "imaginary" pain—along with his imaginary fist grabbing my nuts. Was this a flaw in Crawford's reasoning? I wondered. But best not goad him with that presently.

"What do you think you saw?" I asked instead.

"I thought I saw . . . something leave this old woman's dying body, something else gather it up and . . . a final destination," he murmured.

"You think you saw death, take her soul . . . to where exactly?"

"Let's find out, shall we." he said, brandishing a second lattice from his workbench and hurrying into the refrigeration room. A moment latter he wheeled out an examination table carrying a covered body.

"You stole a dead body?"

"Why not, there's refrigerated semi-trailers full of them in back of the Clinic. And this is the same old woman I

33

watched die. Let's see what you get from her." It was only then I became absolutely certain Crawford was insane. I suppose anyone else would have known long before, but at that moment, in that basement, I felt quite crazy myself.

Crawford uncovered the body (I had seen her before, in the hospital, still alive), wheeled her up next to me and placed the brain lattice carefully on her head.

"Breath slowly and concentrate," he said. "This may take some time. She is cold and dead after all." I struggled to relax but slowly a fuzzy image appeared in my mind. I saw a pleasant landscape—a green field, some trees, blue sky and white fluffy clouds.

"Yes!" Crawford crowed. "Exactly what I saw. What would you say it is?"

"A memory, her home, somewhere she wished she was instead of the hospital?"

"It's Heaven Minh—the after life! I've proved it exists, although I don't expect a heathen like Nguyen Le Minh to believe it."

"Jesus Christ, talk about a leap of faith. This proves something—but not that!"

"Let's bet your life on it." Crawford sneered, snatching the brain lattice for his own head and rolling the dead body away. He disappeared behind me again and soon I felt the sting of a needle in my shoulder, some surgical tape and the cold flow of an IV into my veins. "We'll make this gentle my friend, the IV will stop your heart beat very slowly," he said, sitting back in the chair opposite mine and adjusting the brain lattice on his head. "You and I will watch together. The mystery of life, death and eternity revealed at last."

"We'll both die Crawford! What can you learn from that?" I screamed.

"I don't think so—I'll pull the IV if needed. You'll still have to die of course—I doubt you'd ever forgive me. There'll be no pain to speak of, but you may lose consciousness before the end. Never fear, I will record your sacrifice for posterity."

I tried to thrash and squirm out of my restraints to no avail, then spewed a mad string of expletives at Crawford until he responded by gagging my mouth. "Relax Minh, agitation will only make your heart stop sooner. I can feel how weak you are already."

Despair gripped me. I saw no escape, and gagged I could not even beg for my life. Crawford no longer saw me as a friend or fellow being. I was an experiment, a personal achievement. He felt nothing for me, even with the help of his brain lattice.

Then, in total surrender, I remembered Crawford mentioning "consciousness" and thought about what that meant in the Buddhist teachings of my Vietnamese, refugee family. Consciousness was all that we ultimately are—all that passes through the Bardo of death into re-incarnation.

I began to meditate as father had so diligently taught me, to control my breath and mind, to narrow my vision to one calm point of single focus, the point of oneness, the point of no self, the point of connection to the all.

"What are you doing?" Crawford's angry visage floated up from beyond. "Stop that. Fight for your life! I can't move—you're draining me." He was a distraction, a dream from a world I no longer wished to know. The Tibetan book of the Dead spoke of these hungry ghosts—these distractions pulling the dying astray. They are not real. They are illusions now.

"Minh, Minh stop—my heart—I'm afraid—something's coming for me." Wake up Minh, please. I'm paralyzed, I can't reach the IV. Please Minh, you're killing me!"

But "Minh" was no longer. No longer in this realm of illusion. The stages of death had begun. The earth, the basement, his former existence turned into water. The water, the emotions, the memories, his attachments turned into fire. The fire turned into air, into peace, into freedom, into unity. The air into consciousness, pure, eternal, unchanging.

The forty-nine days of the Bardo are for choosing, if not ready for Nirvana, then for return to Samsara. A time to learn, a time to choose, a time to seek fortunate birth, a time to follow Karmic winds toward a happy womb, a time to be reborn.

* * *

I am honored to record here the words of Rashmi Lakmal on the approach of her tenth birthday. Untutored in ways of the west, her knowledge of English and the places and matters of this story appear miraculous in our eyes and to the ears of all those honored by the hearing of them since first she began to speak.

The people of Sri Lanka believe and honor the teachings of the venerable Buddha. We believe in reincarnation throughout the many realms of Samsara. We celebrate the great blessing those who recall this journey provide for guidance in the completion our own. As is our tradition, once recorded the teller never dwells on a past life again, but diligently strives to gain merit and knowledge in this life to help in their next journey through the Bardo.

Rashmi Lakmal knows little more of the people of whom she spoke, but feels the one called Crawford now abides in a place of great conflagration.

Weekdays and Saturdays Gregor and Simon worked at the Ferrous P & T scrapyard on Aetna road, an unsightly, ancient junk emporium gnawing on the metallic bones of Cleveland for generations.

Thingamajig

Gregor Dombrowsky was foreign born, well educated by his immigrant family and clever with his hands. His family's initial success between the world wars withered after the swinging sixties along with their Cleveland machinery business and neighborhood. By the twenty-first century Gregor was just another old codger scraping by with social security and menial labor. But he was still rather exceptional—among the passionate few happily obsessed by otherwise, questionable enterprises.

From early youth Gregor felt called to the collection and study of humanity's manufactured refuse, the unwanted gadgets and gimmicks discarded along the winding road between invention and obsolescence. Such castoffs were not garbage to Gregor. They were pure, rust-brown gold that could be stripped clean, melted down, and repurposed into more and better of the same. He dedicated himself to pedaling this discarded, material ephemera forward into an unknowable future.

"Where you get that, Browsky?" Simon asked one evening in the dilapidated, green bungalow on Crofoot Ave. they both called home.

"Lee Road," Gregor snickered. "Smack-dab in the officious, kosher heart of The People's Republic of Cleveland

Heights."

"We ain't allowed to trash pick no tree-lawns up there," Simon said. "Why you risk that when you knows better?"

"Because it spoke to me Simon. Look at it. Have you ever beheld anything so intricately complicated and functionally mysterious?"

"Guess not," Simon said, giving it a wary look-see from the kitchen stove where he was frying up their supper. "It look electric, but it ain't got no plug. What do it do?"

"Who knows?" Gregor mused. "But I cannot wait to find out."

* * *

Weekdays and Saturdays Gregor and Simon worked at the Ferrous P & T scrap yard on Aetna Road, an unsightly, ancient junk emporium gnawing on the metallic bones of Cleveland for generations. Gregor ran the scales where overflowing trucks loaded with metallic trash arrived full and left empty.

Differing metals earned escalating prices, simple iron was worth the least and copper and brass the most. Empty truck weight was subtracted from fully loaded weight and payouts calculated per pound. Loads with differing metals had to be weighed, unloaded and reweighed multiple times. Gregor found such repetition soothing and delighted in the complex calculations that resulted.

Simon worked the scrap piles, waving in each new truck and showing them where to unload. Being several decades younger than Gregor and educationally allergic to the math involved in price per pound and empty from full, Simon endured the year-round assault of Cleveland's weather outside and wore out six pairs of work boots a year.

They ate lunch together, seated on a filthy bench in Gregor's office and talked of nothing but copper, steel, aluminum and iron. They formed a family of sorts, a balance of strengths and weaknesses, a marriage of inconvenience. But in this neighborhood of lonely, beaten-down men, shuffling about their grimy business amid forgotten factories, warehouses and train tracks of a once proud city, they were not unhappy with that arrangement.

"I seen good stuff t'day," Simon whispered. "Electric motors full o' copper—dumped'm high, so they rolls down back o' the pile."

"Excellent," Gregor whispered back. "We shall abscond with some tonight on departure."

"Once the boss man get gone?"

"Most assuredly, my larcenous, Nubian compatriot."

"What the hell, Browsky, when you gonna learn to talk real American?"

* * *

After work, this unlikely pair prowled the streets and back alleys of the city, always one strategic day ahead of garbage collection. Of course the amateur trash pickers (arthritic codgers toting somber bouquets of black, garbage bags, and babushka'd crones pushing rickety shopping carts), had already gleaned the easy, aluminum cans while Gregor and Simon worked at the scrap yard.

Serious scavengers like Gregor and Simon hunted the heavy stuff (discarded washers, stoves, lawn furniture and auto parts) that could fill a pickup truck and earn meaningful cash. Gregor would pilot their rusty Ford pickup alongside the curbs while Simon popped open garbage can lids and pawed through household trash heaps on foot. A good evening would earn them both the price of a restaurant supper. A bad one just cost them some gas.

Sundays the two would sit out in their squalid backyard drinking beer, near an illegal bonfire burning the insulation off tangles of copper wire and sending pungent clouds of black smoke into the urban sky. Simon traded food and beer for this wire every evening with his gang of local, underage "wrecker boys" who snuck into abandoned buildings to tear copper wire from walls and ceilings. In a way Simon mentored them, replacing absent fathers and incarcerated, older brothers.

To Simon this hardscrabble life was about daily survival, lottery tickets and an occasional tryst with one of the local ladies who sold romance by the hour. For Gregor it was both a vocation and obsession, feeding his insatiable curiosity in the unwanted possessions of others and ongoing quest for the perfect, castaway "discovery."

Every night while Simon retired upstairs to enjoy rescued movies and music, Gregor would descend to the basement workshop where he deconstructed, studied and occasionally repaired anything sufficiently enticing, complicated or rare. Currently the focus of this intense productivity was his mysterious Lee Road find. Occasionally Simon would look in to scrutinize and kibitz.

"What you call that?" Simon asked.

"I'm uncertain," Gregor said. "I suppose it's a machine—although of unknown purpose. Perhaps mechanism or instrument would be more accurate? Artifact? Specimen? Object? Even organism possibly? You're the poetic soul among us, Simon. What would you call it?"

"I calls it a waste o' time," Simon said. "Who need this thingamajig anyways?"

"THINGAMAJIG—that is perfect!" Gregor crowed. "Everyone wants a Thingamajig!"

Simon did not share this opinion. He knew old white folks get crazy from time to time. There was no stopping them from going off the deep end, so it wasn't worth his trouble to try.

* * *

Upon inspection, the "Thingamajig" resembled a metallic insect or spider. There was nothing remotely organic about it, but diverse attachments and protrusions were vaguely reminiscent of legs or antennae. It weighed roughly three pounds, but considerably more when dampened during cleaning. Obviously what appeared solid, even armored in some sense, was also curiously absorbent.

"Crack it open." Simon said. "Pull the guts out n' see what's up inside."

"Easier proposed than accomplished," Gregor sighed. "These exposed fasteners will not accept any common screwdriver or wrench. The whole assembly appears foreign made."

" Oh I knew that," Simon said. "Them China-men use secret commie glue on all their stuff. Let me fetch my ax from back by the woodpile. I'll split this sucker open in no time."

"Not yet, thank you! I believe we shall research the matter further—before resorting to gross nuclear options."

"You go do whatever, Browsky. I ain't got no money on it."

At which point Simon left the discussion and retreated upstairs to watch Caddyshack, which they recently rescued from a local garbage can on VHS tape. Simon had a wide array of cast-off amusement upstairs, all rescued or repaired by he and Gregor. He could indulge in vinyl records, cassettes, eight tracks, CDs, DVDs, VHS and even Betamax. They had yet to unearth an elusive, vinyl, movie record and player, because those were exceedingly rare and commercially unsuccessful even when new.

After laborious modification of screwdrivers to match devious slot patterns, Gregor succeeded in loosening a pair of small fasteners on the Thingamajig that might offer logical points for electrical connection. It was a wild guess, but beat the extreme option of hatchet technology. Attaching a substantial cord and three-prong plug, Gregor stepped back a considerable distance, readied a fire extinguisher, put plug into socket and flipped the power switch.

A loud POP and FLASH plunged the basement into darkness. When no fire ensued, Gregor switched it off and employed a flashlight to locate the household breaker box. At the same moment he heard Simon's loud, plaintive lament.

"Damnation! Why n' HELL you shut off the power, Browsky?"

Upon resetting the appropriate breakers, all of which had flipped simultaneously, the house lights came back on—precipitating an even louder racket upstairs. "Holy crap Browsky, get your ass up here toot-sweet!" Somewhat alarmed, Gregor turned to grab the fire extinguisher, but stopped short in amazement. The work bench was totally empty except for the charred remains of the power cord. The Thingamajig had completely disappeared. After searching the area and finding nothing, Gregor was startled to hear Simon clomping down the stairs.

"What you waitin' for old man?" Simon howled. "You hear me bust-ah-gut or no?!"

"I was searching for our Thingamajig," Gregor sputtered. "I believe it has disappeared!"

"Oh, you does, does you? That ain't half of it, Browsky! Get your dumb ass up here!"

The two scuttled back upstairs and into Simon's cluttered media room. Gregor saw nothing amiss besides the usual masculine, grubby disarray of their abysmal housekeeping.

"Well?" Simon said, hands on hips indicating an unusually, perturbed mood with his portly, elder partner.

"Well what?" Gregor replied warily.

"Does you got EYES, Browsky? What you gonna do 'bout that?!" Simon shouted, pointing to the ceiling while actually hopping around the floor in agitation.

Looking up, Gregor was astonished to see the Thingamajig embedded upside down on the ceiling—four or five of its vestigial appendages piercing the cracked plaster like metallic claws.

"Did it crawl up there?" Gregor said, eyes wide with disbelief.

"How the HELL does I know?" Simon growled. "You turned the damn lights out!"

Aside from the obvious conundrum of how an inanimate bundle of wire and metal moved almost instantaneously from the basement to upstairs and why electrical current should trigger such a reaction, Gregor had two further issues to ponder; did it not look somewhat larger and heavier hanging ominously overhead? And who should be compelled to retrieve it? However, Simon had a rather determined response to that negotiation.

"That be all on you, Browsky."

"You are the taller one among us Simon, just reach up and grab it."

"Oh no, you woke it up. I'll fetch a chair n' baseball bat—in case it get feisty." Gregor mounted the dining room chair with some reluctance. Bracing himself with one hand on the chair back, he reached one hand up under the core of the Thingamajig. Meanwhile Simon stood ready to bash away at the slightest provocation. Finding his grip, Gregor pulled.

The Thingamajig held firm until the surrounding plaster gave way in a white explosion of dust and shards. Simultaneously, mechanical appendages released from defying gravity and snapped shut like some alien bear trap on Gregor's hand and fingers drawing visible blood. Gregor screamed, falling backward off the chair into Simon's arms.

Baseball bat, Thingamajig, chair, victim and rescuer all rolled chaotically around the plaster covered floor.

Simon recovered first, grabbing his bat and preparing to smash the Thingamajig attacking his friend, but Gregor stopped him in mid-swing. The object had released on its own, Gregor's hand was cut, but not badly mangled and his blood on the metallic exoskeleton of the Thingamajig was quickly being absorbed as if required for nutrition.

"I guess it was hungry," Gregor said, squeezing a few more painful drops onto his strange new pet. Simon backed away in disgust to go find clean bandages and iodine.

* * *

Subsequently, with sufficient incentives, the Thingamajig began to exhibit an array of new tricks and tendencies. It could dissolve and then reappear virtually anywhere. It swam around in the bathtub as if naturally aquatic. Its size fluctuated for unknown reasons, becoming minuscule or enormous depending on the space available in whichever crevice or area it choose to materialize.

Simon was at first appalled by the lengths to which Gregor indulged their new roommate, but warmed to the intrusion when the Thingamajig learned to perform and communicate. This it accomplished via the multiple screens and speakers in Simon's media room.

At first mere video static and white noise were produced. But eventually, after a bit more experimentation, demonstration and blood loss, the Thingamajig became proficient with all available content and learned to take verbal requests.

"Thing-ma-jig, show us the Real McCoys," Simon would say, and up would pop an episode with Walter Brennan and Pepino jabbering away about rural predicaments in which neither Simon or Gregor had the slightest interest. They could suggest a tune, in any genre, from folk song to operatic aria, and one or more speakers would begin warbling a cappella in robotic voices akin to Robbie the Robot or Alvin and the Chipmunks.

"It doesn't seem able to produce actual music," Gregor noted.

"Might be we needs more of them," Simon said. "To whip up a proper band."

* * *

A more disturbing development involved the voluntary opening up of the core of the Thingamajig like an empty, beckoning tube sock. Inside could be glimpsed numerous moist, swaying fibers and tiny, twinkling lights. When comfortable openings formed on both ends and a side orifice like a thumb hole, Gregor dared to cautiously stick his right hand inside.

The Thingamajig fit him like a glove. After some initial jabbing pain at his wrist, the sensation became quite soothing and then actually empowering! Gregor had stumbled onto the ability to direct the power of the Thingamajig to perform wonders at his command. Like Green Lantern's power ring, Gregor's living glove could levitate objects, turn electricity off and on and even cause furniture to vanish and reappear elsewhere.

"You some kinda super guy now," Simon declared. "Like Spider-Man, but old and fat!"

"With great power comes great responsibility I suppose," Gregor mused.

"You gonna wear tights n' fight evil?" Simon asked.

"Heavens no. Half of what we do ourselves is not exactly legal."

"That's good, cause I ain't gonna be no black, Boy-Robin for no old, white fool."

Gregor's enhancement did not prove completely advantageous. He could not pull or order it to come off, and when trying he experienced searing pain at his wrist. Thereafter Gregor hid the Thingamajig under an improvised cast at work and in public. On the positive side, he could still drive the truck and levitate anything heavy off tree lawns and into the truck with zero exertion.

Still, the living glove seemed to drain Gregor and he began to retire early—too tired to putter about in his basement workshop. Simon became worried about his health and wondered if they should visit the local free clinic.

"How is that possible?" Gregor lamented. "They will see my beautiful Thingamajig and try to remove it."

"That's just what you needs Browsky. That spider glove's been eatin' on you."

"Never," Gregor shouted. "I would rather go to my grave than give up its power!"

"You gotta big, bad bug old man. If not on you hand—sure nuff in you head."

* * *

As if rewarding Gregor's loyalty, the Thingamajig grew greater in power and size. It now covered his entire arm and manifested the ability to create favorite foods, drinks and even substantial cash directly at his bedside. He lost both the need and ability to work simultaneously, which Simon found alarming as their life together began to unravel.

"You gotta get up outa this damn bed, Browsky, whiles you still can."

"Why Simon, to keep you in lottery tickets and whores?" Gregor barked. "Go on with your shabby little life, and leave me enjoy mine. Take the old truck, it's yours. You can stay only until the end of the month. From now on my dear Thingamajig will be my best friend, roommate and faithful servant."

Simon was crushed, but too proud to show it. He spent that night drinking at the White Mountain Club on Aetna Road, drowning his private sorrows—although it was the kind of racist, neighborhood dive where he was soon to become unwelcome without Gregor at his side.

The whole history of their time together was foggy in Simon's memory. Had they met at work? Did an arrest for trash picking in Parma and a shared, overnight jail cell begin their decades in tandem? Did they ever discuss what they meant to each other, or the terms of possible separation? Simon could not recall, but he felt the loss deeply. Gregor had been like a grandfather, and Simon like his bodyguard in the worst neighborhoods of their city. The next day Simon begged to room with a frequent whore who often hinted she might prefer a sustained relationship.

Work was a disaster. Gregor had failed to call in, prompting the boss to take his place at the truck scales. Everyone grilled Simon about the old man's absence and implied the younger man was to blame for Gregor's failing health. Some even implied a romantic breakup between the pair which they described as "a little too clingy for friends."

Simon did not even know where to eat lunch, who to talk with or what to do with the empty hours between closing and bedtime. Instead he cruised their usual pre-garbage day routes in the Ford pickup, too sad to gather scrap alone, but unwilling to break habitual routines.

A week passed and then two. Gregor never showed at work and Simon missed his cozy, media room on Crofoot Avenue. He drove down this one-block street early one evening to see if Gregor was home. All the lights in the green house were out and no curl of smoke rose from the chimney, although it was chilly outside and everyone else had their furnaces running.

When Simon pulled up to the stop sign at Crofoot and East 81st, an elderly neighborhood lady scurried out of the house on the corner bundled in a threadbare coat and slippers to rap with her knuckles on his driver's side window.

"Oh, Mr. Simon," She pleaded. "What on earth has happened to old Mr. Dombrowsky?"

"Got me," Simon said, rolling down the truck window. "I don't stay there no more."

"Oh, we know that, dear," she said hesitantly, probably finding it strange to use such an intimate term with a black man. "The whole neighborhood misses you something awful."

Now it was Simon's turn to feel strange. He'd never spoken a word to this white woman for fear of scaring her silly. He didn't even know her name and the "whole neighborhood" she spoke of consisted of four run-down houses, two sagging garages and one boarded-up machine shop that used to belong to the Dombrowsky family thirty-five years ago. The very fact she knew his name and noticed his absence was something of an epiphany for Simon.

"Is he sick? Did he die or move away?" she worried, wringing her gnarled hands around a dish towel from the sink she apparently just abandoned.

"Tell you what," Simon said. "I'll swing round n' check. You go on inside now n' don't worry. I got this—old Browsky n' me go way back."

Simon backed the truck down the street to the green house. The old woman hurried back inside, no doubt apprehensive about the appearance and outcome of her intrusion. Once in the driveway, Simon blew the truck horn three times to see if any lights would come on inside the house in response. Nothing happened, and Simon began to experience a tight, nervous feeling in his gut.

He got out of the truck and tried the side door. It was locked, but he reached down and removed a loose brick from the foundation and there was the hidden door key—just like always.

Opening the door, Simon shouted into the stairwell that led down to the basement and up to the kitchen. "Hey

Browsky, alright if I comes in?" There was no response. The air inside was stale and cold. In the kitchen there was no hint of food preparation or eating, no water in the sink or refrigerator running. Simon prepared himself for the worst and moved down the hallway past his old media room and toward the bedrooms.

Gregor was in bed, covered up to the chin with heavy, wool blankets. There was uneaten food and beverages covering the floor and the night stand held piles of money, both in coins and small bills. Gregor himself looked bad, real bad, drawn and haggard with a rough growth of beard, but still taking shallow, rasping breaths.

"Is that you Simon?" He whispered through dry cracked lips.

"Yeah, I come back for my stuff," Simon lied. "How you be, Browsky?"

"Thank God," The old man sighed. "Don't let me die like this."

"Okay, let's get you outta bed." Simon said, pulling away the blankets to reveal his friend entombed inside the huge, engorged Thingamajig from neck to groin—his exposed legs and feet withered and useless. "What the Hell!" Simon cursed. "How do I get you out?"

"I don't know, I can't move, I can't even see now," Gregor sobbed. "Kill it Simon, crack it open like you wanted—even if that kills me."

"That really what you wants, Browsky?"

"Yes, please . . . and hurry."

"Okay then," Simon said, and went to fetch his ax in the back yard where he used to chop up wooden pallets for their bonfires. Outside he met a group of his wrecker boys standing wide-eyed around the pickup in the driveway.

"Corner lady says you be back," the boldest among them said. "Can we help, Simon?"

"You bet," Simon shouted. "Go run n' fetch the cops n' ambulance. Browsky's dying!"

"Cops don't never listen to us," another boy said.

"You make'm fuckin' listen!" Simon swore. "And don't none of you dare come in this house till I says so. Now get!" The boys scattered, Simon found his ax, but when he tried to re-enter the side door he found the way barricaded with piles of heavy furniture filling the stairwell.

"So that how it gonna be, Thing-ma-jig?" Simon roared. "Well do your worst, you devil—cause I'm-ah-comin'!" Simon spun away from the blocked door and smashed the nearby kitchen window with his ax—jumped up on the truck bed and dove through the shattered window frame to tuck and roll over the kitchen counter and onto the glass strewn linoleum. When he stood up cupboards and cabinet doors began to spring open and disgorge their contents in his direction.

The Thingamajig was powerful, but Simon knew this house and kitchen well—because it was his very home. He grabbed the old, ironing board stuffed in alongside the refrigerator and used it like a shield to block oncoming torrents of crockery, glassware and cutlery.

The loudspeakers in the media room began to blast the sounds of explosions, gunfire and profanity from old movies in Simon's collection along with improbable song lyrics like "Hit the road Jack, and don't you come back no more, no more, no more, no more!" and "We will rock you—rock you!"

"That all you got?" Simon taunted. as he careened down the hall toward Gregor's bedroom.

The Thingamajig changed tactics, pelting him with wads of paper money and showers of coins while switching to lyrics like "Money makes the world go round, the world go round, the world go round" and "MONEY—it's a hit. Don't give me that do-goody-good Bull Shit!"

Simon reached Gregor's bedroom door and splintered it with a tremendous blow from his ax, knocking it clean off its hinges. As he burst into the bedroom, the Thingamajig quit the bed and began crawling around the walls and ceiling like a mammoth cockroach with Gregor still entombed inside. The speakers in the media room began to scream "Help, murder, no, no, please stop!" and blare the shark theme from Jaws.

Simon took aim at the mechanical appendages that kept the abomination moving. At each chop of his ax the speakers would shriek out the shower stabbing-squeals from Alfred Hitchcock's Psycho. The Thingamajig was now writhing around the floor, flailing its broken appendages with Gregor trapped inside and apparently still alive. Simon stomped one foot down upon the Thingamajig to hold it steady and raised the ax high over his head with both hands, preparing to rescue his friend Gregor with one carefully placed death blow to his captor.

Simon's blow came down, the Thingamajig vanished and the ax blade buried itself in Gregor's chest. Simon shrieked in horror, the cacophony from the loudspeakers stopped and Gregor, with an expression of both terror and relief, took his final, painful breaths.

"Did you get it?" he gasped, as Simon held his dying friend close until the last.

"You bet, Browsky," Simon lied.

All the food and cash that had littered the bedroom floor disappeared. The dishes and silverware that had rained down on Simon were now stacked neatly in cupboards again and the furniture blocking the back stairway vanished to reappear where it belonged in other rooms.

Simon carried Gregor's limp, withered body out of the house and straight into a crowd of Police, EMTs, neighbors and wrecker boys waiting outside. They had heard everything blasted over the loudspeakers inside. The EMTs took Gregor and tried to save him, but failed. The police arrested Simon at the demand of the neighborhood corner lady who loudly swore she had seen him carry the murder weapon inside.

* * *

Simon was convicted of murder (as he confessed giving the death blow), but was declared insane as he was unable to prove anything concerning his mad ravings about the Thingamajig and what happened inside the house. The green house, Ford truck and all Gregor's worldly belongings (which had been secretly willed to Simon anyway), were sold off to pay for his lifetime confinement in a private institution for the criminally insane.

A smallish Thingamajig later materialized intact among

the leftover trash from Gregor and Simon's house, where it was picked up by the wrecker boys who found it inter-esting . . .

T h e   E n d ?

The Cleveland Clinic treated me with
all the deference and attention due a
member of Saudi Royalty, to whom
they famously were known to cater.

Tainted

They were all over my Facebook feed; services called Helix or Life Source that analyzed your DNA, rendering a percentile map of where your distant ancestors originated, including the smidgen of Neanderthal genes still hiding within your genetic profile. I had no interest in discovering any degree of caveman-ship, but I was keen on finding out my ancestral affinity to Scotland.

Father always claimed we were descended from lowland Scots, located north of Hadrian's Wall in the wetlands around Carse Bay and Loch Kindar, but south of the highland clans. There was no "Mac" in front of our name although my mother's maiden name sported a "Mc"—more probably Shanty Irish than kilted followers of Bonnie Prince Charlie. I suspected this supposed heritage was simply dad's excuse to be cheap, or "a wee bit thrifty" as he would say with a bogus brogue.

I paid the small fee, swabbed my cheek, and sent in my sample as instructed. While waiting for the results I discovered Internet trolls denounced these "genetic spies" as government or corporate conspiracies gathering data for future policies of racial control, manipulation, or elimination—unhappy prospects indeed. But I'm not the suspicious type and find unlikely dystopian paranoia amusing. In any event, at sixty-six years old, humanity's future would not depend on me. Mine was a dead-end genome, as neither my older sister nor I had offspring by that point and were highly unlikely to reproduce before our inevitable departure.

Of course I could have gone the genealogy route. There were Internet services and databases of that sort also. But I was too lazy for researching out along the withered branches of my family tree, although mother's family claimed some hope of connection to Billy the Kid. As romantic as such speculation might be, I felt no desire to prove kinship with pirates or highwaymen and considered my forefathers to be more likely cabbages than kings. I find it rather odd, that those who profess knowledge of past incarnations were always Roman generals or Egyptian queens in former lives, instead of village idiots and guttersnipes.

My upcoming analysis of origin held no hope or dread for me. Mere curiosity would not kill this complacent cat. In truth, the entire endeavor faded into mental oblivion by the time my fated hour arrived. My surprise was greater yet, as it arrived not via FedEx or email but by a ringing of my doorbell followed by the polite but persistent rap of knuckles on my front door.

The trio on my front porch might well have been census takers or Seventh Day Adventists, so scrubbed and proper was their smiling presentation. A young man and woman of startling cosmetic appeal were accompanied by a bearded elder practically glowing with the aura of competence and gravitas.

"Mr. Webb?" said the distinguished, older spokesman.

"Hello," I stammered. "Did I win the lottery or something?"

"Yes, in a way," he joked. "We're here to present your genetic profile."

I opened the door and they trouped inside with folding tripods, display screens, and all the hard and soft ware required for an epic sales pitch. There was no-way-in-hell the pittance I laid out for this service covered the overhead of such a lavish presentation. I resolved to hold onto my wallet with both hands.

"Please make yourself comfortable," cooed the comely female presenter. "This will only take a moment." Settling into my easy chair, I watched their preparations with growing interest. A world map and color-coded pie chart took up the tripod spaces while a computer screen was positioned before me.

"Before we begin," the young man said, "are you familiar with the basic concept of a DNA sequence?"

"I think it's like a blueprint for a human being," I said, "and everyone's is different."

"Yes and no," he said. "All living creatures have one, but many of the elements found in the simplest organisms are also found in the most advanced. The complexity of the human genome has developed over many millions of years. While there are slight variations in each individual, like hair color, height, sex, and facial features, everyone's entire, genetic record carries identifiable traces of all their ancestors both human and otherwise."

"Otherwise?" I gulped. "I have non-human DNA in me?"

"Everybody does," the bearded leader said. "You and a banana share a majority of identical genes—but they are arranged completely differently—which makes all the difference."

"We're ready Doctor Marcus," said the female team member.

"Excellent," said the doctor, as he handed me a hefty packet of printed material. "Here is your complete genetic read out. It is yours to keep, and you may read it at your leisure. We are here to explain the highlights and answer your questions. Now, I'm sure you are eager to begin."

It was quite an afternoon. Each section of their pie chart corresponded to an identifiable percentage of the stuff that made me up, and to a location on the world map where that particular variation dominated. Predictably, a large percentage came from the northern British Isles and Ireland. Smaller percentages filtered down from Germany, Scandinavia, and France, with a slight touch of southern European Neanderthal below two percent. Surprisingly there were also tidbits of Native American and even African American. I comically attributed those to the Confederate shenanigans of my mother's folk below the Mason-Dixon line.

This all appeared innocent enough with a few surprises, but nothing worthy of the elaborate in-home presentation I received. My only question concerned their math. The various ethnic percentages, of which I was composed, failed to reach one hundred per cent. My admittedly rough calculations found them deficient by nearly nineteen per-cent.

"Very observant, Mr. Webb," said the doctor, jumping on this opportunity. "That is why we are here today. My assistants, Paul and Miranda, will explain."

"Ever since the complete computer sequencing of the human genome," Paul started, "we have discovered gaps and . . . irregularities in world-wide human sampling."

"It is possible," Miranda continued, "the evolution of modern man was not as linear as we once believed. It may, in theory, have been . . . *collaborative*—for lack of a better word."

"Collaborative?" I said.

"Interbreeding, Mr. Webb. We would call it intermar-riage, but we are uncertain if this mixing was consensual or otherwise. But please go on, Paul."

"Several distinct sub-types have surfaced, including the recently discovered Denisovan strain of pre-Cro-Magnons, which is dispersed primarily among Asian and Pacific Is-land populations," added Paul.

"And then, of course, the persistence of entirely un-known alien influences cannot be entirely dismissed," the doctor finished.

"You mean I have extra-terrestrial DNA?" I shouted. The doctor's eyelids fluttered momentarily. His two as-sistants tensed visibly during his brief silence.

"I would not go that far," he said. "We are focusing our current research on the possible contributions of certain *vanished peoples.*"

This is where their laptop came into play. They showed me multiple world locations where ancient races and civilizations, recorded in the myths and legends of neighboring, historic populations, flourished in antiquity and then completely disappeared. The legendary Continent of Atlantis and the marauding "Sea Peoples" mysteriously threatening the Mediterranean coast of Africa during the time of the Egyptians and Hittites were prominent examples.

"We theorize," Doctor Marcus said, "unexplained sequences in the DNA of living individuals like yourself are vestiges of these vanished populations. You, in particular, live in the area of the lower Great Lakes, where the local Erie tribe of Native Americans were reportedly exterminated by the Federation of the Iroquois for questionable reasons shortly before white men penetrated this region."

"Questionable reasons? What does that mean?" I said.

"Well, we really do not know. The Erie were said to be different, *impure* if you will. They were the only North American tribe to use poison arrows and worshiped different Gods according to the surrounding tribes. But we cannot know for sure because they were all gone before Europeans could verify any of it."

"Then how could I have their genes?"

"We doubt they were all killed," Dr. Marcus explained. "Women and children were likely enslaved and others may have escaped to allied, non-Federation tribes to the South and West. In any event, your genome shows Native American influence. In addition, the Pict tribes of Scotland, who were vicious adversaries of the Roman legions occupying Britain, and a major reason for the building of Hadrian's

Wall completely across the island from the Irish Sea to the North Sea—vanished entirely before the English dared venture beyond the wall a century later. Your nineteen percent genome gap may be a lucky combination from both these vanished peoples."

Oddly, I was not feeling all that fortunate.

* * *

The Cleveland Clinic treated me with all the deference and attention due a member of Saudi Royalty, to whom they famously were known to cater. It was a leap of faith to accept Dr. Marcus' offer of a free, comprehensive physical, but the current ruinous cost of American medical insurance made it seem worth the trouble. After blood work, urine and stool samples, x-rays, MRI, and CAT scan, Doctor Marcus stood beside my bed, in a private room on one of the top-most floors, with a conflicted demeanor.

"You are in excellent health for a man your age," he started. "But we found nothing qualifiable as *special.*"

"Annoyingly average has always been my super power," I joked.

"Yes, well, we hoped to find some internal indications of your unique genetic variation, but I am afraid very little stood out."

"Very little?"

"Small flaps of skin which might close off your ear canals under pressure. Have you noticed any particular discomfort when flying in a plane or swimming?"

"No, but then I don't know what other people feel."

"True enough," he said. "Your ocular bone structure appears larger than normal and there are . . . extensive membranes of some sort . . . on your lungs."

"Cancer? I used to smoke in college."

"No, no, more like a thin, enveloping, scar tissue . . ."

"I had pneumonia several times when I lived in Northern California."

"That might explain it . . . we would have to open you up to be sure."

"I'm not doing that!" I said.

"No, of course not," he said. "You are perfectly free to go with an absolute clean bill of health." This seemed my cue to exit, but Dr. Marcus lingered at my bedside tugging at his beard in a contemplative manner. "We would however," he finally said, "like to offer you one more opportunity."

"Here it comes," I shuddered.

"Actually, it is something many people do routinely, as a matter of charity or civic duty. We would like you to formally will your body to science, after death."

"No way! I know people do it on their driver's licenses, and I respect that—but I'm way too superstitious to have chunks of me living on in other people."

"This would not be organ donation, Mr. Webb. We would simply do an autopsy, under controlled, scientific conditions, recording what we found, and then pay for full funeral expenses in the faith, manner and cemetery of your choosing."

* * *

Eventually I signed the donation papers. I'm not the kind of person who thinks too far ahead: no cemetery plot, no living will, and no written instructions to anyone about final wishes. So it was a blessing to have all that planned out for me. I tried not to think about the ultimate price.

"Are you out of your fucking mind?" my brother-in-law yelled over the phone. "They're gonna cut you up and stick you in jars of formaldehyde. Rich, college punks will have scalpel practice on your heart. They'll shove TV cameras up your ass."

"Actually, they already have," I said. "You're over sixty-five Carl, have you never had a colonoscopy?"

"No-way-in-Hell my wife, your own sister, is gonna sign any damn *donation* papers or give up her DNA sample! How dare you send those creepy-ass grave robbers after her!"

"They're scientists Carl, not grave robbers. They're just doing an important job. And I didn't send them! I mean, I guess I should have realized they'd be interested in my sister, but I didn't give them my permission or even your address."

"You think the government doesn't already have that?" he said. "Do you ever watch Fox News? If I was you I'd go to the cemetery right now and check on your mom and dad—make sure they're still underground."

"Come on Carl, be serious."

"You be serious! It's about time you woke up to what's going down in this country. I can't believe you'd sell your own body for a stinking pine box and six feet of dirt. I knew Janet's family was cheap—but not that GOD DAMN cheap!"

* * *

So yeah, there were unintended repercussions. I'll probably never speak to my brother-in-law again. The jury's still out on whether that's a detriment or a benefit. The way I see it, when you're dead, you're dead. What does it matter who fiddles with your remains? If my name did appear in some research paper or textbook, it would be more immortality than I've ever achieved by myself.

Fairly quickly I discarded any thought of it, along with the packet of unread genome papers I'd received. I went back to enjoying the rest of the summer like all the members of my family had before—boating and fishing on Lake Erie.

On the way back from the North East Yacht Club one night, I took Lake Shore Boulevard through the shoreline community of Bratenahl. I was tired of dealing with the weekend insanity of I-90, so I often go this way. If you know the area you can picture the way the thick tree cover and the gated estate walls of Cleveland's old aristocracy create a seclusion unknown elsewhere in our city. I had the dark, twisting, two-lane road all to myself when it happened.

Without warning the bumper of some huge truck plowed through my passenger side door. There were no warning headlights, no horn, no brake squeal, and no intersection of which I was aware. The terrible, jolting crash sent projectiles of steel and glass exploding around me along with my airbags and whatever torn vegetation I rolled and careened into after impact.

I remember staring motionless into the night sky. Maybe I had been thrown from my car or maybe the collision tore my roof off. The truck backed up and turned its lights on. Somebody got out of the passenger-side of the cab with a flashlight and walked toward me. The truck geared up and roared away. Apparently my little Mazda had barely scratched it.

The guy standing by my wrecked car watched the truck leave and then gave me a kick in the ribs. I grunted in pain, too dazed and battered to form any words.

"God damn it!" he growled. A pair of headlights approached through the darkness along with the rumble of a powerful engine. It all transpired within the slow-motion, dream-like field of my battered perception. The sounds of car doors opening, the shadows of two more figures silhouetted in headlights, and the face of . . . (was it Paul?) floating over me, shining his flashlight in my eyes.

"He's still alive. What should we do?"

"Get him into the ambulance, of course. The longer he lives, the less refrigeration we'll need. Miranda, help him with the body."

There was a great deal of pain. They didn't put me onto a stretcher or administer any sort of first aid, but simply pulled me free of the wreck and dragged me into the back of their vehicle. They rolled me onto a bunk and strapped me in for the ride. There was no siren or flashing lights, just voices from someone driving, (Doctor Marcus?) a man in the passenger seat, and a woman sitting in back with me.

They were wearing EMT uniforms but seemed in no hurry. I could not tell where we were going. Maybe I slipped in and out of consciousness. The next thing I remember was the feel of the ambulance grinding to a stop.

"What's wrong?" said the woman in back.

"We can't see to drive another inch. Where the hell has this fog come from?"

"We can't stop here," she said. "If the police see us it will ruin everything."

"Not necessarily," said the driver. "We simply claim we're rescuing an accident victim. If we are discovered you will have to give him the lethal injection. We can't allow him to talk to anyone."

"Very well, Doctor," said the woman from the darkness surrounding me.

There was a long moment of inactivity as the idle of the powerful engine echoed in the surrounding, murky fog. Then the front windshield imploded into the cab, spraying small chunks of safety glass all over the interior of the ambulance. A short, dark figure wielding a crowbar smashed the glass panels on the back doors and two more diminutive attackers bashed in both side door windows.

The driver swore and stomped on the accelerator, hurtling the ambulance into the opaque, surrounding fog until hitting an ivy-covered, stone wall. Damp, oppressive fog rolled into the vehicle filling every inch with drenching, wet darkness. I heard some random cries for help and a good deal of choking coughs before I blacked out.

* * *

"That should feel better," said a warm, unfamiliar voice somewhere above me. "Can you answer me now, Mr. Webb?"

"Yes," I moaned. "Where am I?" An overhead light clicked on illuminating the inside of the ambulance where I was still strapped onto one bunk. Everything inside was dripping wet, but bandages were now on my arms, my leg had a temporary splint, and I wore a neck brace. I must have been given some powerful painkillers, because I wasn't feeling much of anything. On the opposite bunk sat an attractive, female EMT technician with smooth, olive-toned skin; strange, glistening dreadlocks; huge, almost iridescent green eyes; and wide, blue lips. Between us, three silent, naked bodies lay piled on the floor. They looked suspiciously like Dr. Marcus and his young assistants.

"What happened to them?"

"They drowned in the fog," she said with a sly, cold smile.

"In the fog?"

"It's called dry drowning—quite unusual but very lethal. Are you alright?"

"I've been in two car accidents tonight. So no, I'm definitely not alright."

"Believe me, neither of those events were accidental. Try to relax. My men will have this ambulance back under way in a few moments. I'm agent Marina Vaarg from GLIPS. We'll be taking care of you from now on."

"GLIPS?" I stammered.

71

"Great Lakes Interspecies Protection Service," she said. "You fell into the enemy's trap, Mr. Webb, but luckily, also under our protection."

"I don't understand."

"You will in time. You may even join us in our work—being uniquely suited to blend in ashore." Two squat figures dressed in ill-fitting EMT uniforms climbed into the front cab and we began to move again. I could not see who they were, but neither spoke as we gathered speed and the cold night air blasted through the vehicle from all its missing windows.

"Have you never wondered about your heritage and your name before the DNA survey?" Marina asked, by way of passing time and relieving my anxiety.

"How do you know about that?"

"We have our ways. The *underside* of Cleveland is more plugged-in than you might imagine. What can you tell me about your father's family in Ohio?"

"I don't know much about them. My grandfather was an orphan from Ashtabula. His entire family died in an epidemic."

"I wouldn't bet on that being true," she huffed. "Our people have been persecuted and hunted down for thousands of years, including in the twentieth and twenty-first centuries."

What our people? I thought. *I'm not Jewish or anything.* "My Father said the name Webb came from making fish nets back in Scotland during the Dark Ages."

"Then it would be *Webber* or *Webbers*—there's a difference." At this she held up one slender hand and spread her long, pale fingers wide, displaying the light, vestigial webbing between them. "See," she said, grinning broadly through rows of delicate, pointy teeth.

We drove through the night for some time until arriving at an unknown lakefront. I could hear waves hitting the beach and sand crunching under our tires. The two figures up front got out to push as Marina climbed into the driver's seat.

"Don't worry," she said over her shoulder. "We'll be safe soon."

"From who?"

"Our natural enemies—it's been a long, hard struggle, but our day is coming. Global Warming, Mr. Webb, means less snow and ice, more water, and much less dry land." As the ambulance began to flounder in the lake, water poured in through the missing rear door windows and rose up to where I was still strapped into my bunk.

'Hey, where are we going?" I shouted, straining to keep my head above water.

"Under water where we'll be safe."

"But I can't breathe under water!"

"I wouldn't bet on that either," she said, laughing.

73

I tailed her westward from the Art Institute, past the retail monoliths along Euclid Avenue, around the dark, cubic Museum of Contemporary Art and right up to the oldest house in University Circle.

TES HOUSE

lest remaining structures in
l section. built circa 1853
ure left in the neighborhood.
ew Cozad, the first section
e two-story, one-room-deep
ned a large portion of the
rcle. Justus Cozad, Andrew's
orked as a railroad super-
r section on Mayfield Road
are surviving example of
ture, including a hipped
brackets, and prominent
tional Register of Historic
nd Landmark in 2006.

NC.
OCIETY   87-18

Vanishing Point

"What do you think of this?" Jeff asked, at an inconvenient moment in our shared apartment, when I was chained to my drawing board sweating out a presentation for work.

"What is it?" I said, in a manner I hoped would brush him off.

"A drawing by one of my female students at the Cleveland Institute of Art."

"What's her name and are you trying to know her better?" I said, implying he should leave well enough alone because there are strict rules about that—which he's skirted previously.

"Just look at it will you, Gilman? There's something very wrong here."

So I did. The picture wasn't bad, just a black and white pencil drawing of somebody's room. It wasn't exactly realistic, but not abstract enough to register as unique.

"Give her a C+ and call it interesting," I said, handing him the drawing back over my shoulder. He grabbed it from me and shoved it right in front of my face again.

"You don't even see it do you? It's right there, jumping off the page."

By now I was beyond pissed, but to get Jeff out of my

room, if not my life, I took a closer look at the damned thing.

"Have you taught them about perspective yet?"

"No," Jeff admitted. "I wanted to see where they were on their own first."

"Well then, that's the problem. These walls are slightly curved. The ceiling is all wonky as it slants downward until they all meet at this weird corner. The room's geometry is all wrong. It all kind of makes you feel as if . . . as if . . ."

"Exactly," Jeff whispered as he crouched down to view it at the same angle as myself. "I think she's found what you've been looking for."

* * *

My artistic nature is like a disease, both in a mental and emotional sense. Others have life obsessions with culturally-approved paths to fulfillment. Being artistic is different. It's like a void appears in your soul. It must be filled by something, but you don't know what. At that quivering moment, I hoped a girl I had never met, might provide the answer.

Miriam Bates was a show stopper—if your tastes skewed toward the freakish. Her skin was so pale you could almost see through her into some emptiness inside. Her wispy, platinum hair and the clothes she wore were ethereal. Only the jet black of her shoes and eye shadow held her existence in play. Jeff finagled my "chance meeting" with her at the Art Institute.

"Happy to meet you," she said, without the slightest hint of pleasure. I immediately wondered, are Albino Goths going to be the next Gen-whatever fashion trend?

"Professor Clark showed me your drawing," I said, needing some vector of connection.

"Oh, why?"

"Because he and I share an apartment and I'm working on something similar."

"Oh . . . why?" she said, her tone of disinterest seeming borderline pathological.

"Well, because I'm designing a project you might be interested in. Let me buy you a coffee in the cafe, and I'll tell you all about it."

"I don't drink coffee. It keeps me from dreaming."

Starting out like that with Miriam wasn't very promising, but at least she sat in the cafe listening inertly to my vivid explanations of the Neverland project.

"This project will be like an indoor Disneyland, as re-imagined by Salvador Dali and M.C. Escher," I said, "a visual, sensual playground for stoners. Places like this are known collectively as 'interactive art installations.' There's one named Otherworld in Columbus and a bunch of them called MeowWolf, in cities out west. I thought Cleveland needed one of its own."

The project was an art student's dream job—or should be. I was one of twenty local artists, craftsmen and technicians involved. Artistic license was wide open at this planning stage, so after baiting my hook I cast the lure. "Would you like to join us, Miriam?"

"I can't," she said. "My parents are coming back for me."

I quickly explained she didn't have to go anywhere right now. She could meet the group this weekend, or even participate online.

"Oh, why?" she said. "What do you want from me?"

"We need your artwork, like the drawing you did for Jeff . . . I mean Professor Clark."

"The drawing of my bedroom?" she said, as some first dawning of interest flickered over her otherwise absent expression. "Yes, I draw everything I see there."

"Could you show me more of your drawings?" I said, with a bit too much enthusiasm.

"Yes . . . if mother and father approve." Then she rose to leave, stopped, turned, and looked down at me as if seeing me for the very first time. "Do I know you?"

"Yes," I said, a bit perplexed. "I'm Walter Gilman, we've been talking for over an hour."

"Oh . . . Happy to meet you," she said, and walked away.

* * *

My next move requires some explanation, and forbearance. I followed her home. I'm not normally a stalker, but I could not afford losing my tenuous connection to her authentic genius. Her drawing was rather childish—but its effect was hypnotic!

That quirky little corner, the weird curve of walls and bizarre slant of ceiling, sucked me into her drawing, into her room and into that reality like a blown-out window in a jetliner flying hundreds of miles per hour—like the obese villain, Goldfinger's lacerated, fatal exit in the James

Bond film. I wanted that level of raw, visual magnetism in Neverland.

I tailed her westward from the Art Institute, past the retail monoliths along Euclid Avenue, around the dark, cubic Museum of Contemporary Art and right up to the oldest house in University Circle. This red-brick mansion was built before the Civil War. The historic marker in the front yard said it was part of the Underground Railroad. It is called the Cozad-Bates House. So that, and Bates—her last name, matched up. I thought this place was run by the University as a sort of museum, but to my surprise, Miriam walked right up to the front door and went inside. I thought, Maybe her family still lives on the upper floors?

Once again, I beg indulgence and plead temporary insanity, because I went up to the very same door and knocked to gain entrance. But the door was locked. A sign on the door's window gave notice of closure for renovation. Looking through several other windows, I thought I saw an interior gutted to the studs and door frames—completely uninhabitable.

I wasn't doing any drugs that day, but Miriam's appearance, demeanor and disappearance had me thinking maybe I was having a flashback. Still, I didn't freak out. When I occasionally walk on the wild side, I know how to keep my cool. Subsequent events proved this peculiar talent absolutely necessary.

As I loitered on the porch of the old mansion, trying to ascertain my relative state of consciousness, the front door opened and there stood Miriam, as nearly translucent as before. There was even a barely perceptible breeze, gently blowing past her into the otherwise sealed mansion. It fluttered her ghostly, white hair and clothing with an alluring motion.

This was yet another solid reason to cut and run. However, when finding myself in an ominous, unsolicited, twilight zone—I'm surprisingly tolerant of "special effects."

"Oh," she said. "Do I know you?"

"Yes," I said, determined to flip her script. "You are happy to meet me. You want to show me your drawings."

"The drawings of my bedroom?"

"Yes, I'd love to see that bedroom."

"Oh . . . yes," she said, turning to go deeper inside the mansion. I started to follow, but she stopped and looked back at me again. Her dark, sunken eyes (not eye shadow after all), raked me over from head to toe.

"I don't do sex there." she said, with a strong hint of disapproval and suspicion.

"Nor should you—at your age," I agreed.

"I'm older than I look," she said. "Much older."

Once inside things got weirder. The mansion's interior was not gutted as I observed earlier, but dripping in quaint, antique craftsmanship and furnishings. A sepia glow clung to everything as in very old photographs. Obvious time warp, I thought, or really dirty windows? Dust lay thick all around. My fingers traced noticeable trenches up the bannister. Miriam left no shoe prints whatsoever on the steps as she led me upstairs. Very light on her feet, I guessed.

From outside, the mansion appeared to be two stories with a full basement and high mansard roof, topped by a low-windowed belvedere skylight. But once inside, the stairway climbed at least four flights, each veering left off a landing and each narrower then before. We crested at a square foyer the size of the skylight overhead. Three doors led off to left, right and straight ahead—behind us being lost to the last staircase. "Which room is yours?" I said.

"You choose, they're all mine."

I chose the door directly facing the stairs, promising a marginally quicker escape.

The door opened out, and we went in. Immediately I recognized why her drawing looked so bizarre. This room, and likely the others also, scrunched down under the descending roof line and wedge-segmented the attic floor level into three, radical slices of architectural pie.

There was a dormer with a tiny window sunk onto the room's exterior wall and vertical walls that rose up over ten feet toward the center of the house but tapered down to five toward the outside. It was like stuffing rectangular reality into a triangular universe. Plus everything: floor, ceiling, and walls exhibited almost two hundred years of accumulated sag and settling.

"Charming," I said, "very cozy."

Miriam had me sit down on her single, iron-frame bed and fetched a thick roll of her drawings from a tiny desk and chair shoved under the window in the dormer. She sat next to me as I unrolled them. Her lack of training in perspective was glaring. There were no horizons, no vanishing points to which all horizontal lines should flow, and objects didn't shrink or grow to indicate distance.

But this flaw was not universal. Only a few of her "works" dealt with the bedroom. The rest were filled with things and places unknown. The terms abstract or visionary were inadequate to describe what I saw—hallucinogenic or demented might be closer. There was little need for perspective in the boundless, surreal realms she brought to paper.

"You said you draw what you see," I said, trembling. "Where do you see all this?"

"Oh . . . up there." she said, pointing to the corner where ceiling met the walls . . .

When I looked up at that corner, the infamous corner that brought me here, my mouth fell open. Miriam's drawings rolled back up on themselves and fell off my lap. I stood and stumbled forward, placing my hands on the faded wallpaper. "You see all that right here?" I said.

"I see it through there."

"May I see it also?" I said turning to face her, but we were no longer alone. A tall, older man and a short, matronly woman now stood beside Miriam. All three looked bleached out, colorless and spectral. I shuddered, as Mom and Dad were apparently back . . . possibly from the long departed.

"Did he hurt you?" the old man asked Miriam.

"No," she said, "I want him to see." Then all three raised their arms and ran toward me. It felt like their hands sunk into my chest as they slammed me against the wall—then through it! Terrified, I thought the fall would kill me, scramble my brains out against the flagstone walkway below, but there was neither above nor below. I was floating in a dark, unexplainable expanse and my brains were scrambled completely.

* * *

I wish I could describe the teeming chaos existing beyond our comfortable three dimensions. Perhaps if I fell from those feverish realms back into our own reality, life would be just as overflowing with terror and wonder. Alas, my mind is insufficient to grasp such probabilities.

At times I was not myself, but a floating cloud of sentience tethered to my past by a silver thread reeling out behind me, like a spider plunging from the top of a skyscraper. I felt propelled forward by my own volition and the will of three guides—two bigger clouds of iridescent bubbles and one smaller, crystalline entity shooting out beams of golden light in all directions.

The cyclopean cities we passed through, the monstrous entities we escaped, were legion in the infinite realities stacked like decks of cards in our path. But always we flew on, led by the crystalline guide and the wild, chaotic music of the void. At last we approached a scathing realm of fire, ruled by a gigantic, horned deity, black as volcanic glass. His numberless followers rained in from all directions to crash down, searing their names in blood upon his molten registry, then dancing off in a frenzy of damnation upon his vast dance floor of burning coals.

I am no church goer, but I'm familiar with the literature. This was not a tango I wished to join. Signing in blood was my deal breaker. Instead, I reversed trajectory and reeled back my silver thread with urgent velocity. Who knew salvation was that easy? "Just say No," indeed!

* * *

I awoke on the wooden floor covered in broken lath and plaster dust. Miriam's bedroom was empty, no bed, desk or chair, only a jagged hole where the corner had been. I dragged myself up and peered back into the hole. Inside was a rough, sealed-off void between the inner walls and outer roof and a thick roll of drawings on yellowed paper.

I stuffed the roll inside my shirt and made my way downstairs. The mansion interior was now gutted for renovation again and all exits locked. I fished out my cellphone (apparently unfazed by being through all Hell and back), and called the University Circle police.

"How'd you get in here?" the officer said, as the front door was unlocked to let me out.

"I came in to see a young woman's drawings," I said, with slim hope of being believed.

"Was her name Miriam?" said the grinning maintenance man assisting the officer.

They gave me the whole story, along with a citation for trespassing. They said the total University Circle area was haunted by ghosts (mostly students who committed suicide after spending all their parents' money, then failing exams), but especially by Miriam Bates.

The Bates family were into Spiritualism—holding seances, talking to the dead, and Miriam was their medium. Although she was very good at it, she wanted to be an artist. A rich industrialist wished to make her his mistress, trying to rape Miriam in her bedroom. The entire family disappeared the next day. That was a hundred years ago, but Miriam often reappears at artistic events. The Art Institute lists her as a student in memoriam. Sometimes she attends class.

* * *

Despite, or possibly because of my recent supernatural odyssey, the planning for Neverland accelerated. Miriam's drawings became central to the overall project. Guests would enter through a child's bedroom, which would be huge, distorted and disproportionate—making adults seem lilliputian. They could exit in a myriad of ways and directions; climb under the bed, enter a closet, be swallowed by a giant toy, ride an escalator through the ceiling or walk into a mirror.

From there, other choices led to more and more surreal environments, many suggested by Miriam's drawings or my experience. Each of these realities connected to others or even back to the bedroom. Round and round and round they could go, and when they stopped . . . well, that depended on fate, bladder control or closing time— whichever came first.

Of course there were difficulties. Disney threw a hissy fit about the name. We changed it to Forever Land, which seemed more positive anyway. We built the whole thing in a bankrupt, multi-story, department store, like a monstrous Spirit Halloween. Everything had to be fireproof and washable (some vomiting was expected). We positioned exits at reasonable intervals and hired "rescue rangers" to roam the many realms to comfort the severely lost and confused.

It was all good. The opening sold out for a solid week. Thousands of folks gave us rave reviews on Yelp. I even met Miriam wandering through the crowd one night. She still didn't recognize me, but was just as unconvincingly "Happy to meet you."

In retrospect, I should have known. I was the last to leave on opening night, but there was still an empty car in the vast parking lot. Great, I thought, somebody hooked up and left together, even though I didn't consider the Forever Land experience particularly romantic. It wasn't more than eight weeks before the investigations and lawsuits began. As it turned out, for every thousand people who paid admission, about half a dozen never came back out.

Carley and I came to view the desolate remains and maybe pick over some bones. One particularly impressive carcass is the rusty, metal skeleton of the Sidaway Pedestrian Bridge.

The Bridge

Sidaway Avenue doesn't amount to much anymore, just two short scraps of pavement on either side of a dark, yawning ravine. Hundreds of people lived around here once. Two entire neighborhoods have been lost to time and urban blight. They're all swallowed up now by "The Opportunity Corridor."

I call it a ruin crawling—exploring what's been lost and what's left behind. There are many dying, urban neighborhoods in Cleveland, but few more moribund than this area. Someday the Cleveland Clinic will expand again and gobble all this up. Carley and I came to view the desolate remains and maybe pick over some bones. One particularly impressive carcass is the rusty, metal skeleton of Sidaway Pedestrian Bridge.

"You can barely make it out," Carley said. "It's like the trees and vines have taken over."

"Imagine how invisible it is in Summer, when everything's covered with leaves," I said. "If it wasn't still on the map you'd never find it."

The map was an old, county map put out by The Commercial Survey Company. I doubt they even exist anymore. You won't find this place using Google maps—but the bridge itself has a Wikipedia page, with a twisted history, early drawings and black & white photos.

"Let's have a look," I said, exiting the car. "Take some pictures and try to cross it."

"What about my new car?" she said.

"We'll park and lock up. It's not like there's any traffic."

"In this neighborhood Jeff, are you crazy? It will be dark soon."

"It's not that bad. And look, there's nobody around anywhere."

"That's my point," she fumed. "This is just the kind of place they dump the bodies."

"What are you worried about, Baby? I'm the white, fish-out-of-water here."

"And I'm the nice, black, college girl from Cleveland Heights who'll be found raped and murdered next to your dead, white ass. Now get back in this damn car!"

Carley and I have been tight ever since we met at Case Western Reserve's all night Fright Movie Festival. We're both seniors. She's a serious med student and I'm a some-what dutiful business major. It's a bit of a challenge for our families, but we fit together really well in private—if you know what I mean.

The glitch is my addiction. "My death wish" as she calls it. I rock climb, sky dive, race dirt bikes and explore abandoned buildings—for kicks. Carley gets nervous and doubts my sanity. On the brighter side, she can set broken bones and close gaping wounds, which might come in handy. So, on this occasion, we left the bridge undisturbed, but I knew I would return alone—prepared for adventure.

Eventually Carley agreed to drop me off near the north

end of the bridge, spend her morning in University Circle, and pick me up when I called. This was no easy sell, because she learned the ravine was actually Kingsbury Run, site of Cleveland's infamous "Torso Murders."

Ignoring the "Buddy System" isn't smart for ruin crawlers. Folks fall through rotted floors or get buried under collapsing ceilings. But without some element of danger, why do it? You gotta man-up to earn serious "Indiana Jones" credit with my buddies.

The north end of the bridge featured steel barricades, chain link fencing, and tangled trees, vines and pricker bushes. With the small machete hanging from my belt, it would take an hour to cut through, and draw unwanted attention. Instead, I went over the edge of the ravine and attacked the bridge from below. Its' wooden decking burnt away long ago, the open, metal spine of the structure hung above me. I had only to climb up a vine-encrusted tree trunk to gain access.

With a little effort I found myself on the only suspension bridge in Cleveland. Like a miniature Golden Gate, it hung gracefully from two towers much taller than the trees. I thought it might be dangerously corroded, but the elderly structure seemed solid. Only the lack of flooring threatened me. I had a heavy coil of rope and mountaineering clips to deal with that. I took some selfies with my phone to impress Carley later, and started across.

The first hundred feet went slowly. I worked out a system of hanging onto one rusty railing, crab stepping along the solid beam of the same side and clipping and unclipping to the small cables running down from the suspension yoke hanging between support towers. It was a difficult routine but prevented falling. The ravine side dropped away swiftly below me. To loose my grip or stumble meant serious injury or even possible death below.

As I cleared the first tower, roughly a third of the way across, another danger arose. I was feeling nauseous, dizzy and a bit confused. My eyes were watering, going in and out of focus and I thought I heard voices from below. *What the hell is happening?* I wondered, sneaking a glance downward. *Oh my God, there are buildings and people down there.*

In shock, I released one hand and twisted to scan below—but my right foot slipped off the beam and should have plunged down through the open grid work. It did not. The wooden decking of the bridge floor was now solidly in place. Astounded, I crouched down to feel the weathered wood. Just then I was engulfed by a choking blast of acrid, black smoke from below.

I'd never experienced anything this bad, much worse than strong wind blowing through a smoky bonfire. Coughing and choking on my knees now, I pitched forward and peered over the other edge of the bridge floor. There was a train passing below me—pulled by a steam engine!

Nobody ran steam engines in this day and age except amusement parks. *Was I dreaming?*

The engine moved away and its' smoke cleared. I stood up, dumbfounded at the expanse of wooden walkway now stretching to the south end of the bridge. And unbelievably, there was an amusement area there—an outdoor beer garden with live polka music and people dancing.

This could not be happening. The area was deserted,

the bridge impassable. I had to be hallucinating. *Carley was right,* I thought. *I'm going insane.* I calmed myself; studied my surroundings, felt the wood planks underneath me, listened to the distant music and voices. *WWJD = What would (Indiana), Jones do?* He would check it out of course, and I did also.

I unhooked my safety clamps, coiled my rope and tried to look presentable. I hid my sheathed machete down a pants leg and walked forward. *Carley will never believe this.*

By the time I reached the beer garden I had a theory. Either the bridge was some sort of time machine, or I had already fallen and lay in a coma at the bottom of the ravine. *No problem* I decided. *Either Carley calls the cops and EMS to rescue me or I've become the new H.G.Wells.*

Old Mr. Wells took my early bets. There were no synthetic fibers visible. Only cotton, wool and leather apparel surrounded me with precious little English being spoken. I knew this area was called "Slavic Village" full of Polish, Slovak and Czech immigrants. But it became mostly Black after white flight emptied Cleveland's east side in the 1980's. I'm no expert, but this crowd looked Eastern European, Great Depression chic to me. I was time-tripping for real.

"Who this face?" a burly Polish bartender asked, pointing at my retro t-shirt.

"Ah, David Bowie?" I said. "Probably not your kind of music."

"What you drink?" he growled, missing my joke by over forty years.

"Ah, just some bottled water please." I said, before regretting my time bias again.

"No water—beer!" he grunted, filling a huge glass stein from a wooden barrel.

I'm not a heavy drinker, and this stein probably weighed like three pounds. It was also unrefrigerated, lacked the surgeon general's warning and contained unknown alcohol content.

"You pay now." he said, before I could take another sip.

I almost used my debit card, but caught myself and offered up a fiver and change.

"Not America money!" he bellowed after close examination. "You try cheat me?"

"No, no, it's absolutely American, " I said. "Just not quite yet."

I desperately searched for something to pay with after he threw my funny money back in my face. Pulling the machete from my pants, trying to barter . . .

"Robber!" he yelled to the entire place. "Help get gangster boy!"

Luckily the wooden bridge deck made escape easy. I hoped it extended all the way to the north side and called Carley on my cell phone as I ran—but there was no signal. The phone was working but had no cell tower or satellite service. *Of course not* I realized. *I gotta run all the damn way to the Twenty-first century!* Mercifully, the bridge decking continued, but not that far.

At the north end, the barricades, fencing and foliage was gone, but so was the landscape where or when Carley dropped me off. Instead I found a run-down neighborhood of wooden housing—some boarded up and some needing to be. The air smelled of smoke and tear gas. The sound of gun shots and police sirens seemed just out of sight. *The nineteen sixties* I guessed. Hough riots, bussing, white flight and once again I'm literally on the wrong side of the tracks. *I'm not even born yet*, I thought. *How do I get back to Carley? How does this time warp work?*

A large group of Black men appeared about a block away. They were marching, chanting slogans, carrying clubs and torches. They were breaking windows, kicking down doors, searching house to house. One marcher stopped, shouted and pointed. They were mad as hell at somebody, somebody who probably looked a lot like me.

Turning tail, I ran back south on the bridge; felt the nausea and dizziness again, knew I passed through the time warp—*but to when? Did going south regress in time and north jump forward? If I go too far will the decking vanish or the entire structure cease to be?* I wracked my fevered brain for some salient Wikipedia updates.

Mayor Tom Johnson builds a wooden trestle span between the Hungarian, Kinsman area and Polish, Slavic Village in 1909. By the mid-1920's the Van Sweringen Brothers tore that down for their railroad to Shaker Heights. Instead they build this suspension bridge in 1930. It becomes the dumping ground for the torso murders from 1935 to 38. Massive white flight happens throughout the 1950's and by the Hough riots of 1966 Cleveland splits into Black and White armed camps. Slavic villagers burn the wood decking to enforce separation. The bridge is closed and abandoned for 57 years . . . so far.

So maybe, I thought, I *could wind up anywhere from 1930 to 2023—unless I stumble into some distant future where this ruin still exists.* "Jesus Christ!" I swore. "How do I get out of this?" At that moment I wished I had fallen off, and lay down below in a coma. At least I could wake up from that.

Trying to decide which way was out, I saw another time traveler slumped on the floor against one railing whimpering uncontrollably. As I approached to help I was jolted by a new revelation. It was Carley—dressed like I last saw her, and beside herself with fear or despair.

"Carley Baby!" I shouted, gathering her up protectively. "What are you doing up here?"

"Freaking out looking for you," She sobbed, holding me tighter than ever before. "What the hell have you been doing for the last nine, God-damned hours?"

"Sorry, it felt like one or two for me. But, I tried to call you . . ."

"I tried to call you—twenty times! I drove back here, to both sides of this stupid bridge. Then I called home for help. My brother and his friends are searching the ravine for your body!"

"Why not just call the police, Baby?"

"So they can arrest you for trespassing? What the hell is happening up here Jeff? Why did I feel sick just before this flooring appeared and why are folks who don't even speak English chasing me away shouting the N word? This is Cleveland Ohio, not fucking Mississippi!"

"I know, I know Baby, it's a lot to process. This is Cleveland, but not our Cleveland . . . and not in our time, not in 2023."

It took awhile to calm her down enough to explain— not that I had solid answers. She had seen enough Twilight

Zone and Multi-verse movies to grasp the concept. Carley's a tough girl when she needs to be. She ordered her brother to boost her up on the bridge while he searched below and she's not fond of heights. She risked that for me, and I owe her big time.

"So you don't know how it works?" she said.

"All I know is between these towers time becomes permeable. I don't know why and I don't know how to control it. It may be absolutely random."

"But it stays put," she reasoned. "We don't go elsewhere."

"We go else-when," I said. "If we stay together I believe we'll arrive together."

"No problem then. I'm not leaving your ass alone again for love or money."

"I appreciate that Carley. I feel the same, but I don't know how to escape the warp."

"I do," she said. "We get the hell off this bridge."

Night was coming on and we didn't want to spend it on the bridge. I could probably go south and survive and Carley would probably be accepted to the north, but we had pledged to stay together and either direction looked like a coin toss.

"Why don't we just jump off?" Carley said, as some sort of dark, desperate jest.

"Hold on," I said, holding up my rope "We both climbed up—why not climb down?"

We peered over the side but saw nothing and nobody who might oppose us. Carly called out for her brother Sam and his friends Tyrell and D'vonte, but there was no response. We were near the center of the bridge, well within the warp zone and according to Wikipedia some eighty feet above ravine bottom. My rope was approximately a hundred feet long and strong enough to hold both of us. I tied a knot in it every ten feet to give me footholds on the way down.

"Are you sure about this?" Carley said, as I tied off one end of my rope to the strongest piece of steel railing I could find. "Don't go showing off and get us both killed."

"If Luke and Princess Leia can swing across that air shaft with Storm Troupers blasting away at them, I can safely lower both of us to the ground. Now climb over this rail, stand next to me and hold on around my neck and shoulder like your life depends on it."

"Okay," she said, and kissed me on the cheek. "Leia wishes you luck."

Our decent was not that hard. Basically I just had to slow our downward slide and avoid major rope burns. I work out, but climbing up double loaded like this would have been a bit too much for me.

On the way down we both felt the warp sickness. I hoped we were escaping its' effect, but half way down the entire area lit up with a whoosh of flickering intensity. Looking up we saw the bridge decking was ablaze. Knowing my rope would burn also, I sped up our decent.

Moments later the rope went slack and we fell to the ground. I twisted so Carley would hopefully land on top of me, but our drop took only seconds. We couldn't have fallen more than eight or ten feet and escaped with minor bruises and dirty clothes. Above us the bridge burned itself out and disappeared entirely in a dramatic mixture of thick smoke and nightfall.

I thought it dangerous to wander around in the dark, so we gathered some twigs and branches and lit a small campfire using the still burning end of our rope. We could cuddle together until morning and then, hopefully, make our way home. The total lack of city sounds seemed ominous and our phones still didn't work. Only crickets and occasional wild life sounds kept us company. I thought we could make-out a little to ease the tension, but Carley was definitely *not* in the mood.

Sometime after Carley fell asleep, I heard footsteps. It was almost morning, but still pitch dark in the valley. Those approaching whispered to each other. I could identify two or three voices, but not the language. I considered dousing our campfire, but had no water. Probably it was too late for that anyway. It had already betrayed our presence. I woke Carley and had her stand behind me. As the others became visible, I placed one hand on my machete.

they were a small group. A man and woman with a baby followed hesitantly by two young children. They appeared to be wearing feathers, shells and animal skins. Native Americans apparently, but not all that far removed from the dawn of human kind.

The man carried a spear tipped with flint and the young boy a rudimentary bow and small arrows. The man stopped with his family behind him, thumped his spear end on the ground, raised his free hand, and uttered something unintelligible.

I released my machete grip, raised my free hand, and

said "Hello friends." The man smiled and waved his family forward. We all gathered around the fire and began to trade looks and gestures. We examined each others' attire, and shared some snack food I had brought on my ruin crawl. The young girl tried wiping the Africa from Carley's arm. Obviously Carley and I were not back home. We were in a place and time neither of us belonged, but possibly both might be considered welcome.

MORE
GORE
from
CLEVELAND

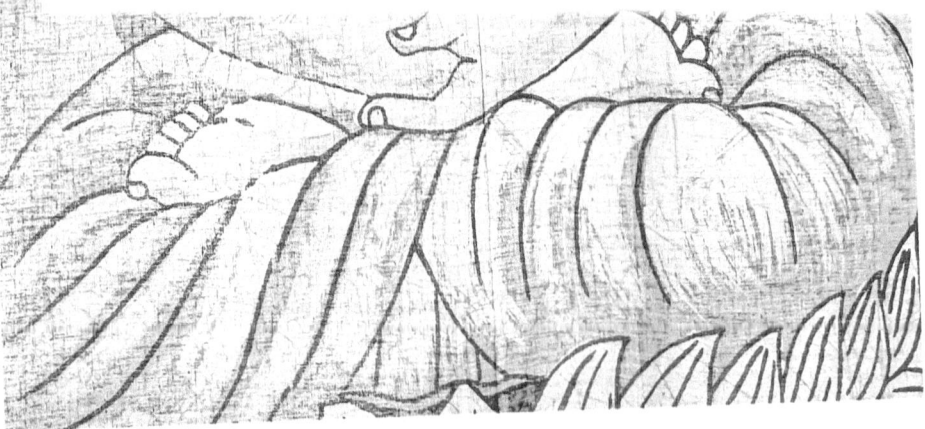

This Unitarian Universalist Church offered a veritable smorgasbord of religious affiliations and rituals, and in truth my wife and I had sampled most of them previously during our wild years of laissez-faire, drug-assisted spirituality in California.

Earwigs

The hiss of an old steam radiator dribbles away in some hidden corner of the room. Sometimes it's barely perceptible, but oddly loud and persistent late at night or first thing in the morning. The trouble is I haven't lived anywhere with steam heat since the nineteen seventies and I certainly don't have such a heating system in my home now.

But there it is, insinuating itself into my most private moments. A sound I know does not exist, but hear anyway. My wife doesn't hear it and consequently is tired of hearing *of it* from me. Of course she has various phantom body pains that no doctor, chiropractor, acupuncturist or massage therapist can locate or quell—and I'm bone tired of *hearing* about them also. But, since she is heavily into playing medical, specialist roulette, I figured I'd consult one myself.

"It is probably tinnitus," the senior audiologist at the Cleveland Clinic said. "Did you ever work with heavy machinery?"

"How heavy?" I somewhat joked.

"Perhaps *loud machinery* would be a better term. Ever work around air compressors or jackhammers? Ever go to a rock concert, shoot guns or get close to a fireworks display?"

"All of the above I'm afraid. I listened to rock music, own an old pistol and still love fireworks. Am I doomed by my prior commission of questionable activities, Dr. Hellmann?"

"We all are, one way or another," he said. "Our prior omissions also. For instance, did you ever use ear protection during these debatable pastimes?"

"The little spongey things you stick in your ears? Hardly ever," I admitted.

"Well, there you are. All those OSHA warnings have a purpose, but we ignore them until age and injury catches up with us."

"Did you ever fall victim to your own misspent youth, Doctor?"

"Absolutely. I never flossed—I hated those ridiculous waxy strings. This flawless smile I am currently flashing— cost me thousands of dollars in veneers and implants."

After the lame jokes and faux camaraderie, the doctor expounded on damaged nerve endings and other unrepairable mysteries of the inner ear. The morning and evening timing of my affliction was about attention vs. distraction and the inward or outward focus of my mind's eye.

"So why not bells?" I asked.

"Come again?" he said, as he prepared to finish with my trivial laments.

"I've been told other peoples' ears seem to ring, but mine hiss. What's up with that?"

The question altered the mood in the examination room. Perhaps the learned doctor had missed this aspect of my complaint? When he turned to respond I thought there was a calculated nonchalance to his face, belying a sudden intensity in his gaze.

"People describe the experience differently," he began, quickly checking my admitting statement. "Are you sure of your own description as . . . how did you originally phrase it, *some sort of wet hiss?*"

"Dead certain," I said, mirroring the aggression of his stare. "In fact its volume is increasing right now, even as we speak."

"Curious," he snapped, as if I struck a nerve. "I'll have to get back to you on that after I review the literature." But, as I was getting off the examination table to leave, he tentatively reengaged with a somewhat, accusatory afterthought.

"Do you ever hear anything else unusual?" he asked.

"Unusual, like how?"

"Like suggestions or requests," he said. "Are you hearing voices, Mr. Carson?"

I have always been a vivid dreamer, in color and often vaguely disturbing even though I can never recall specifics. My dreams have become even more intense since I started drinking *ZzzQuil Nighttime Aid* before bed. I haven't used illegal substances for many decades, due to the annoying onset of government-mandated drug testing, but I've increased self-medication with alcohol and over-the-counter goodies.

I generally get up at least twice a night to pee these days, but fall back asleep almost instantly. Sometimes my dreams involve dialogue, weird music or violent struggle.

I told Dr. Hellmann about all of this and about the occasional hearing of my own name, "John"—as if spoken by some stranger in my room. This wakes me immediately, but nobody's ever there.

The Doctor suggested we should do some recorded, sleeping tests, like those used to diagnose sleep apnea, and that I might seek out some personal counseling.

* * *

"He thinks I might be crazy," I summarized for my wife.

"I could have told him that," she said. "Does he recommend an asylum or lobotomy? You should go for the asylum. I'll be damned if I'm changing your diapers here at home." As callous as this may sound, we've been intimate since graduating from Cleveland State University and have thus honed our contentious, domestic banter to a near-vaudevillian perfection.

The audiology tests at the Clinic were expensive. They were somewhat like an eye examination with those small, flashing lights scattered over a dark grid, but blindfolded now in a darkened room with auditory beeps and bloops of varying tones and intensities broadcast from multiple directions. Dr. Hellmann performed several Alzheimer's tests as well, to gauge my memory—as both my parents succumbed to that horrible, brain-wasting disease.

"You have some significant hearing loss," Hellmann said. "Especially in your right ear. That is common for a man your age. You are right handed, so I imagine whatever noisy tools you used were probably held by that hand and therefore closer to that ear."

"Probably true," I agreed. "And I've long had gunk and fluid build up in my right ear while the other is always clean and dry."

"That is caused by sinus irregularities I believe," he explained. "We would all like to think our cranial cavities are perfectly symmetrical, but that is never the case."

* * *

I undertook my recommended counseling at the Unitarian Universalist Church. It's a benefit available to parishioners. My wife is an over-active member there and occasionally drags me along to holiday services and special events.

This church offers a veritable smorgasbord of religious affiliations and rituals, and in truth my wife and I had sampled most of them previously during our wild years of laissez-faire, drug-assisted spirituality in California. Ping-ponging between Tim Leary, Alan Watts and the Maharishi, scarfing down free food from the Hare Krishnas, while reading Tarot cards and casting the I Ching. We were spiritually promiscuous to say the least.

The church's main pastor, Samuel Clark conducted my counseling sessions—no doubt with an eye toward firming-up my church affiliation and tithe offerings.

"So John, you think you're hearing things?" he said.

"At least that's what they tell me."

"Are you hearing anything right now?"

"Other than my limited time left on this planet ticking

away," I said, "not really."

Clark was unamused with my jocular attitude, but maintained his own pastoral tone and began to speak of historical and biblical references to mysterious messages from the great beyond. I'm familiar with some of these and consider others as literary or mythological preoccupations. I think of most as dreams or ideas concocted within a recipient's over-active imagination. But, I have to admit hearing directly from a *Burning Bush* would be a deal breaker.

"Would that frighten you?" Pastor Clark asked.

"Hell yes," I said. "It would probably provoke more questions than answers."

"And what would those questions be?"

"Why me for starters? Who am I to warrant that kind of attention?"

"Ah, hah," he said. "So you would see actual proof of supernatural contact as a punishment instead of a blessing—very interesting. Do you generally feel put-upon by the supposed interventions of divine will?"

"Absolutely, doesn't everybody?"

* * *

The Clinic's recorded sleeping tests were even more expensive than their hearing tests and required over-night scheduling. I prepared for my first session as I normally did at home, but my Clinic sleepover was monitored, recorded and filmed by an attendant hidden behind a two-way mirror with electronic sensors affixed to my head, neck and body.

This was massive overkill as far as I was concerned, but medical science is a needy, expensive boondoggle.

I thought all the medical preparations would ruin any chance of a normal sleep routine, but within minutes of laying down the hiss returned. *Good,* I thought. *Let's give these science nerds a run for their money.*

Before my first piss-intermission, which usually occurs over two hours after first closing my eyes, I heard my name clearly spoken. I snapped awake as usual, but instead of total absence I was confronted by a room full of lab-coated clinic minions led by Dr. Hellmann.

"Thank God, Mr. Carson," he gasped. "We were afraid we couldn't wake you in time."

"In time for what, breakfast?"

"Before you stopped living! Your brain waves, respiration, heartbeat and blood pressure just fell off our charts. John Carson, you almost died here tonight."

* * *

"I'd sue their damn brains out!" my wife fumed. "I'd hire that scary, Big-Brother lawyer on all those billboards around town. He'd make them pay."

"I'm deeply moved by the intensity of your love and avarice my dear, but nothing really happened. They've tested and retested me like a moon rock. I'm perfectly healthy and they've waived all charges for the test session. So it was a bit of a thrill ride actually."

"Oh whoop-dee-do," she said. "But if you ever scare

me like this again—I'll smother you while you sleep myself."

Outwardly I was completely at ease after the session. After all I'm a motorcyclist, and coming as close to death as possible is a big part of that addiction. I don't want to live forever, but dying of old age in a hospital bed or a dementia facility like my parents was unthinkable.

However, something else about the aborted testing gnawed at me. I recalled a bit more than I let on, and needed to discuss it with someone reliable. But first, I wanted to Google-dive the near-death rabbit hole. I'd never done any real research about mortality, immortality or damnation before and wanted to be fluent in the current jargon.

"What're you worried about?" my wife griped. "You were a Buddhist back in San Francisco. You die, reincarnate, spend a few seasons as a squirrel and start over again—forever."

"Oh, no, no," I said. "I achieve Nirvana, jump off the Wheel of Samsara and never have to put up with any of this earthly bullshit again."

"Not if you take the Bodhisattva vow. After that you're stuck on rewind forever helping all sentient beings reach Nirvana—and there's trillions and trillions of those clueless fuckers."

"I didn't take that."

"Yeah you did. I was meditating behind you. I pinched your ass, but you took it anyway."

"I was probably tripping my balls off at the time—so that doesn't count."

"Ooh-wah-wah stuff counts double when your cosmic

junk is hanging out," she said.

* * *

"Thank goodness," Pastor Clark said, as I returned to counseling. "Your wife told me you recently dodged a bullet."

"So I'm told," I conceded. "I was completely unconscious at the time. Consequently, I doubt I had anything to do with it. Maybe God lent a hand or maybe I won the life lottery—by missing a golden opportunity to leave."

"I assure you that chance will come around again," Pastor Clark said, with a wink of dark humor. "But tell me John, generally speaking, do you feel prepared to check out?"

It was a loaded question. No doubt he felt it necessary to probe for suicidal thoughts in such circumstances and to gauge my enthusiasm for the inevitable. My recent Google plunges had all focused on how to approach or avoid this personal extinction event. I belatedly realized that possessing one single religious perspective might be far easier than touring the vast, belief bazaar currently befuddling humanity. Should I stick to the roulette table in Vegas, or feed every damn slot machine up and down the strip? Which really improves my odds of winning?

"I guess that depends on what I think happens afterwards," I told him.

"Indeed it does," Pastor Clark mused. "Everything we discuss in this building is more or less about what happens next. Lacking a personal faith, most of it is little more than educated guesses and wishful thinking. But I'm not being very helpful, am I?"

"At least you're not selling me indulgences. I'm drowning in wishful thinking! I googled everyone from Amon-Hotep to Zoroaster. I might as well be listening to Earwigs."

"Ah, the old, nefarious Earwigs," he laughed. "There's an unreliable resource. Little creepy bugs roaming the damp bedding of drafty castles and Iron Age hovels. Were they the devil's six-legged deceivers or royal envoys from the court of the Fairy Queen?"

"You know we still worry about such 'bugs' to this very day," Clark continued. "But now they are listening to us—gathering secret information instead of providing any. No revelation means what it used to. Every belief system either evolves or dies off. If one of those legendary, earwigs crawled into your auditory canal right now, what cosmic truth might it whisper to you?"

"About the same as any priest or politician I guess. It's all a blind crap shoot isn't it?"

"I'll never admit to that John—but sadly, for many people, it is a growing suspicion."

* * *

Shortly after this counseling session, I received a text from Dr. Hellmann. He seemed over-eager to resume my sleep testing.

"Are you crazy, Doctor?" I said on my subsequent call. "I'm not into Russian Roulette."

"At least come by the Clinic and watch the recording

from your first session. We were all so panicked by your vital signs we totally overlooked the real data."

"Almost dying seemed pretty real to me, thank you."

"That's my point, Mr. Carson! The test showed you were never in any actual danger. But you did exhibit some extraordinary symptoms none of us have ever witnessed before."

I'm not usually accommodating when offered traumatic encores, but he wasn't charging admission and I had lingering unease about that test. I felt I dreamt vividly, if not memorably, before being awakened, and my residual discomfort over that dream was vexing. So I went back determined to gain some clarity—but not to repeat the experiment.

*　*　*

"I'm glad you decided to come," Dr. Hellmann said. "Clinic management urged me to destroy this data. But, since you are not suing us and we're not charging for therapy, I hoped we could share what we learned. Your recollections may augment our own understanding."

"I'm okay with that," I said. "But I'm not willing to repeat anything that happened in this room." Privately, I questioned everything that had or hadn't happened enough to pack a hidden form of personal insurance—guaranteeing I would not lose control of the situation again.

"Agreed," the Doctor said. "Nothing new will happen. We recorded two hours and forty minutes of test time. Fifteen minutes were of you first falling asleep. Let us show you some of what happened after that." Hellmann and two attendants booted up the equipment in the control room where the technician watched me sleep. An image of me on the bed appeared on the back of the two-way mirror with superimposed read-outs from all the sensors they had attached.

"Looks pretty normal to me," I said.

"It was. These sessions can be deadly dull unless someone really starts snoring or experiences troubled dreams," Hellmann said. "But as you see, you were unusually still— barely even breathing. Now let us adjust the volume beyond standard, clinical levels."

As one technician slowly turned a dial, the vital signs intensified. This wasn't unusual as he was adjusting the sensitivity of the instruments and I soon learned why. My mysterious "hiss" became audible.

"That's it," I shouted, "that's exactly what I've been hearing!"

"That's also way below *normal*, auditory limits," Hellmann said. "We've goosed it up considerably. How long have you been able to hear this Mr. Carson?"

"Five to ten years maybe? My wife stopped sleeping in the same room with me decades ago because I snored so badly, so sometime after that. What's making the hiss?

"It's coming from you. We don't understand how—but that's not all you're doing."

Hellmann ordered increased video speed, turning hours into minutes. He had the audio muted and increased the image size to highlight my sleeping face and vital signs. I began to appear almost frozen, with my mouth slightly open, as my vital signs started to slide downward. There was no rapid eye movement under my closed lids although I recalled dreaming, no perceptible breathing and a visible stiffening of all body parts.

"This is when the attendant thought you were dying," Hellmann said. "He panicked, hit the emergency alarm and woke the entire facility. I and the staff dropped everything and raced in to save you. Nobody paid attention to the monitors after that, but the test was still running."

"So this is just before you tried to wake me up?"

"Yes, possibly six to ten, *normally fatal* minutes late. You must remember how you immediately awoke and reacted as if nothing had happened."

"Yeah, you all looked like you'd seen a ghost."

"We feared we had," Hellmann said. "But in our alarm and amazement—this is what we all missed." The technician carefully rewound the video to moments before my vital signs flat lined, then restarted at normal speed. "Please prepare yourself for a shock," Hellmann warned me, and clicked on the enhanced audio tract.

As the hissing crescendoed, images began to flood back into my memory. *The Primal Iron Door and the Slithering, Slobbering Horrors behind it. The hissing force of malevolence, spewing into our world under the pressure of vile intent.* But that was in my mind, not from the screen. On screen, there was the alarming hiss and then . . . *My whispered chants, the timeless incantations barring the way. The list of Seven Seals, the Locking for Eternity, the Forever Vow, the Flaming Sword no evil can pass. We say these. We cast these spells. We voice the law and prophecy. We guard the Night Gate, We hold against the Tides of Chaos.*

* * *

"Are you alright?," Dr. Hellmann said, helping me off the floor. "We were afraid you might fall back into a trance once you heard those words."

"What words?" I said, appalled at the breach of every sacrosanct practice hidden in normal consciousness even from myself. "I just suddenly felt light headed and lost my balance."

"Those strange, cryptic chants on the tape, you old fool!" Hellmann shouted. "You fell into another fugue state as soon as you heard it. What does it all mean? What language are you speaking? Ancient Egyptian? Sumerian? Pre-Aramaic? I must know!"

"I just fainted, damn you! I'm seventy five years old and only speak English."

"You did not faint and you don't sleep either. You enter a severe trance only observed in Buddhist monks of advanced rank preparing for their death, the Bardo and reincarnation."

"I don't know what you're talking about!" I lied, knowing I must somehow deny and defend the ancient truths most humans aren't allowed to know. "I've got to go home now, got to talk with my wife. I want nothing more to do with all of this."

"You are in grave danger," Hellmann said, directing his attendants to take hold of me. "You are an extremely sick man. I must insist you stay while we perform more tests!" I managed somehow to struggle free, as Hellmann tripped an alarm and the room began to fill with more clinic personnel, who must have been laying in wait for such a moment.

"The fuck I will," I swore, pulling out the old revolver that I usually hide in my car, from beneath my bulky jacket. "I'm going home or maybe to prison, but I'm never entering a hospital or a church again!" Dr. Hellmann and the crowd of attackers backed off as I threatened to shoot anyone trying to stop me. I thought they'd call the police as I careened down long, Clinic hallways toward my car, but preferred dying in a shoot out over revisiting the terrifying release of all that lay entombed in my subconscious.

* * *

Later, after immediate pursuit failed to materialize, I weighed my limited options. If I went home, or submitted to the authorities I would be poked and prodded until I gave up what never must be surrendered. I'd become a lab rat or a captive lunatic at best. I was too old to hide and two weakened to fight. Therefore I must escape, to a state beyond discovery.

I returned to the place prepared for me, my final sanctuary, my place of rest. I must arrive here eventually, lay down my burden and prepare to be renewed and reconsecrated. It was a good day to die.

* * *

Dr. Hellmann was admitted to the private sub-basement of the Clinic to deliver his report before the resident Vaarg executive relaxing in his nutrient, slime pool.

"Here's everything we've been able to learn about John Carson," he said.

"Leave it on my desk, Doctor. I'm not about to read it in here."

"Of course not your Enormity," the wisely, subservient doctor said. "There are still many unanswered questions that need investigation."

"All I, and the Vaarg need to know is if this old zealot, Carson can be forced to break his spells and open the Night Gate?"

"I'm afraid not," Hellmann said. "Mr. Carson shot himself in the head at his family's burial place, sometime after he escaped the Clinic."

"He didn't even try to go home?" the hideous executive wondered. "These old Boomer fanatics are far more dedicated than they appear."

"Yes, and his wife has already lawyered up. It will cost the Clinic foundation many hundred thousands of dollars to keep her quiet."

"Not my problem," said the monstrosity sloshing out of the pool and toweling-off his ghastly appendages with clean, white Clinic towels. "We'll uncover other paranormal sentries, now that we know how they're camouflaged."

"It is a pity the Old Gods were so negligent as to allow human, Axial Age sorcerers to erect these spiritual defenses," the gross abomination mused. "And even worse that we Vaarg underestimated the ability of rebellious, Age-of-Aquarius fanatics to reinforce them."

"I am preparing something for publication in *The Lancet*

and other medical journals your Enormity," Dr. Hellmann said. "I'll call it 'The Hissing Syndrome' or something like that—see who else asks for our help. Next time we catch an old, hippie necromancer, they won't escape."

"See that they don't," the grotesque autocrat said. "We must smash open the Night Gate permanently—before some dangerous, evolving, AI life form discovers religion."

"I offer NASA a sort of insurance policy," I explained. "Human exploration has never been terribly prepared for new discoveries. Consequently we've stumbled into a shit-load of cultural destruction, genocide and plague in that process. NASA would like to do better."

Deep

Frank Reynolds was the young, fortunate son of old Cleveland money, but luxury and leisure were not his style. He was a mover and shaker—currently running a large construction company that worked for the NASA Glenn Research Center and Cleveland State University where I both consulted and taught.

"So what is an archeology professor doing for a space agency?" he asked in the NASA lunchroom one day. "Are you into some sort of ancient aliens bullshit?"

"No," I chuckled. "But I wouldn't totally flush those theories—prehistoric covers a lot more time than humans have documented. In fact, I've recently enhanced my academic resume. I wear my exobiologist hat working over here."

"Is it made of tin foil?" he joked. "Because I don't think the agency's found anything for you to work on—biologically speaking."

"But, this is Cleveland," I said. *Wait Until Next Year* is our civic motto."

* * *

So that was how Frank and I became friendly. He was

a very business/engineering type guy and I am all history/philosophy—"old news & views" as he called it. But we both kept an open mind and enjoyed sharing new experiences. It helped that his family money took us anywhere and provided anything that piqued our interest.

"I offer NASA a sort of insurance policy," I explained. "Human exploration has never been terribly prepared for new discoveries. Consequently we've stumbled into a shit-load of cultural destruction, genocide and plague in that process. NASA would like to do better on the Moon, Mars or anywhere else we step ashore."

"Do you believe we're capable of even imagining what we'll find?" he asked. "I mean most of what went wrong here on Earth has been about greed and prejudice as far as I can see, not ignorance and poor planning."

"Greed and prejudice are ignorance, Frank. If we thought ahead, if we tried to understand, to imagine the consequences before we took action—world history might have been quite different."

"You're too optimistic Professor. Most science fiction I read is not about happy endings. Wishful thinking is usually fatal."

"Agreed," I said. "But we have to try. I myself was caught up in something that happened right here in Ohio—that I'm not at liberty to share. But I can say it involved antiquity, biology and danger. If I'd been smart enough, careful enough, even intuitive enough, I could have saved a life and avoided freezing away a brand new threat to all humanity in a science lab."

I can't say if Frank believed me, but he stopped busting

my chops about working at NASA. He even hired me as "academic backup" for his newest business venture. As a chronically underpaid faculty member, I needed the money.

His company had been hired by a shadowy outfit called Lakeline Corporation to redevelop an abandoned tourist trap in Castalia, Ohio. The place was called THE BLUE HOLE, and was a big deal back in the 1920's and beyond. I remember my grandparents talking about it as some sort of bottomless well of mysterious blue water. Just seven miles south of Cedar Point, it was part of the mid-century vacationland craze surrounding Sandusky Bay.

On first impression, the place seemed little more than a scummy pond. It was maybe seventy-five feet in diameter surrounded by overgrown vegetation next to a gravel parking lot and a shabby souvenir building.

Mr. Webb, the folksy, white-haired representative of Lakeline Corp. said there was never any swimming or fishing allowed as pond temperature was always forty-eight degrees Fahrenheit year round, and the water was anoxic and therefore totally devoid of fish—which was somewhat bizarre because the land was owned by something called "The Castalia Trout Club" since the mid-nineteenth century.

Its water source was assumed to be an underground spring as the pond level never changed no matter the local weather and drained out continuously into a small stream eventually emptying into the Sandusky River.

"Tourists really came to see this?" Frank asked.

"Up to one hundred sixty-five thousand a year," said Mr. Webb. "But that was before television."

"It must have looked better then," I observed.

"Of course," the old man said. "It was a beautiful blue-green color, crystal clear as far down as you could see. Folks called it a bottomless wonder."

"But of course it wasn't?" I said.

"No," Webb assured us. "It was once measured by drop line at sixty-three to sixty-five feet— but is probably a good deal less than that today. It's just a plain old sinkhole gentlemen, nothing strange or magical about it."

The first order of business was environmental clean-up. The thin coating of green scum covering the pond was probably caused by agricultural runoff which recently polluted the nearby Maumee River and western Lake Erie with poisonous algae. Also, the souvenir stand and nearby buildings may never have had more than rudimentary septic systems.

Frank brought in machinery to bulldoze the souvenir stand and rework drainage around the area. He also brought a mobile crane, as there were reports numerous stolen cars were submerged in the pond during thirty years of closure.

"I'd call for the cops to be here while you dredge the pond," I suggested. "You never know, there may be dead bodies in some of those sunken vehicles."

* * *

The day dredging began Frank and I watched from across the pond. The police were present and Frank used a hand-held radio to communicate with the crane operator.

"Raise the claw all the way to the top, Jim; I want you to monitor the amount of cable you use so we know how deep it really is. Extend your boom as far out as possible from the shoreline to reach the middle of the pond."

"Got it boss," his operator said. "Where should I drop whatever I haul up?"

"Just swing around and dump it in the parking lot. We'll let the police check everything before we haul it away."

As the mobile crane approached the pond's edge, I had a momentary premonition about the stability of the shoreline. I warned Frank to radio for the operator to turn the tank-like treads of the crane parallel to the bank at a greater distance, which should place as much weight as possible on solid ground. Frank gave me a jovial thumbs-up on that.

"Keep it up, Professor. You're paid to do the worrying for both of us."

The operator called out footage as his cable lowered the mechanical claw to the pond's surface and then into its murky water. At about fifty-six feet down he reported encountering something solid.

"Grab on and pull it up." Frank said.

The wet cable began to rise from the pond but soon stopped as the crane body tilted toward the water. We saw the crane operator in his cab shifting gears and levers as he tried to free whatever was stuck on the pond bottom. He moved the boom from left to right trying to pry his quarry loose from different angles and directions. Finally he began to reel out and then snap his boom back, causing the entire crane to rock back and forth adding momentum to the effort.

"I don't think he should do that," I said. "What if the cable snaps?"

"Jim knows what he's doing," Frank replied. "He's the best I've got."

"I can feel it breaking free," Jim said over the radio, just as a huge bubble of noxious gas belched out of the pond. The crane momentarily reared backward as if some giant rubber band had snapped. Then, just as suddenly, lurched forward. The boom pulled all the way down into the water, the entire crane tipped over and Jim's screams came from the radio as he tried to escape. In a few seconds the crane was dragged into the water and disappeared beneath the churning, fetid surface.

"Jesus Christ!" Frank shouted, as he and I ran around the edge of the pond. The police and construction employees gathered at the edge as Frank arrived and began tearing off his shirt and shoes to dive in after Jim.

"Don't try it!" yelled the policeman holding Frank back. "You'll never find him in that muddy water."

"He was belted into the operator's chair," another of Frank's employees said. "If he doesn't pop up soon, he's finished." Frank turned to me with a wild look of anguish.

"Were we supposed to imagine this?" he moaned, pointing at the water.

"No," I admitted. "But Webb's claim of *nothing strange or magical* was obviously a very bad guess."

* * *

Chaos reigned at the construction site. A television crew came from Sandusky. Eventually water rescue divers from the Coast Guard began to search the murky depths. Ropes with grappling hooks were thrown into the water to "drag" for a body and an ambulance was summoned. The unlucky crane operator never resurfaced.

"His body won't bloat and rise up for at least two days," a policeman said. "If he got free of the cab." I wondered if he'd bloat at all in such oxygen-starved water.

Jim's family was notified, and a nearby preacher and his congregation arrived and had to be restrained from starting a round-the-clock prayer vigil. Meanwhile, O.S.H.A. and local ambulance chasers began to sniff around for who to blame.

Frank was a wreck. I sequestered him in his BMW while I juggled media, clergy, safety forces and bureaucracy. By nightfall most of this circus departed. I set up a generator and floodlights around the site. The divers gave up, having never found Jim or the sunken crane.

"Visibility is near zero down there," a diver said. "There's a ring of junk around the edge of the pond fifty feet down—old cars, garbage, construction debris, probably dumped in here for decades. It formed a sort of false bottom."

"And the crane tore through all that?" I guessed.

"It must have. Maybe that big bubble everybody saw was trapped gas—methane from rotting garbage or something, that buoyed up the center of the trash layer. Anyway, there is nothing but a huge, jagged hole down there now."

"So Jim, the crane and whatever it broke loose sank

through that hole?"

"They must have."

"How far down does it go?"

"I don't know. Our lights wouldn't penetrate that far. I'm not sending anybody else down there until that ring of garbage is gone—it's too dangerous."

I sat talking Frank down for hours. He seemed a tough guy, but the loss of Jim hit him hard. Of course he felt it was his fault, for not anticipating all possibilities. I'm over a decade older, and somewhat jaded, but I never had to "comfort" anyone until that night.

"You said something like this happened to you," he finally asked.

"Yes, I didn't actually witness it . . . but I was responsible."

"Did it change you?"

"Change me? God no, there wasn't time. We all nearly died—should have died! But afterward, I felt . . . the victim was a very, talented, young man, but foolishly brave."

The next day Frank put me in charge of clearing the vegetation around the pond, fending off the media and removing the underwater trash ring to avoid any further catastrophe. All of this on top of my class schedules at CSU and NASA work.

"Is that all?" I said. "Where the hell will you be while I'm playing Superman?"

"In Florida," he said. "Buying and learning how to operate a submarine."

"You're going to retrieve Jim's body and the crane all by yourself?"

"No, of course not Professor, you'll be coming down with me."

* * *

I planned to slow-walk everything until Frank returned, but Mr. Webb, dropped his genial facade and showed up aggravated and adamant the next day.

"Lakeline Corporation demands this project be completed on schedule!" He said. "Why are you stalling Mister, . . . whoever-the-hell you are?"

"I'm Dr. Samuel Stern, and we're waiting for Mr. Reynolds to acquire special equipment to retrieve the body and machinery from the bottom."

"A doctor running a construction project?" he seethed. "Look saw-bones, Lakeline doesn't give a damn about what's left on the bottom. We want the pond's water restored, the landscaping done and the visitor center completed—ASAP!"

"I'm a scientist at NASA and a professor at Cleveland State University, for your information. Mr. Reynolds and I do care, very, very much, about the unfortunate victim down below."

"Fine," Webb sneered. "We'll allow a nice *commemorative plaque* installed for him if necessary—at *your own* expense."

After that unpleasant exchange, I got Frank's men busy on the landscaping, the parking lot and the foundation of the visitor's center. Meanwhile, I tracked down a maritime salvage company to handle removing the underwater trash ring.

That proved extremely difficult. The sunken cars and debris came up easily. What undergirded this layer required divers cutting away sections with underwater torches. When Frank appeared back in Castalia a month later with the mini sub, we had only removed a third of the ring running parallel to the parking lot.

"Your toy submersible won't be big enough to raise the crane," I said.

"It will be enough to free Jim's body and attach lift cables. Anything bigger couldn't maneuver in this pond." Frank replied. "How's the trash removal going?"

"The parking lot shore is clear, but you should see what we pulled up."

"In those old cars? Please don't tell me you found Jimmy Hoffa."

"No, not Hoffa—but we discovered something fishy." That night I drove Frank to a warehouse in Sandusky. Our discovery was arranged carefully, piece by recovered piece, over the expansive floor.

"What the hell is this?" he said.

"It's copper, apparently woven into long strands up to six inches thick."

"Professor, I mean what is it supposed to be—not what it's made of."

"A safety net I think, to keep stuff from sinking down, or perhaps floating up?"

Its age was unknowable, copper being a metal like gold or silver that tarnished, but did not rust. Copper was used by man's earliest civilizations. Who installed it and when was a mystery. Lakeline said they knew nothing of the original construction. Castalia had no record of costly engineering at the site, only old news clippings with grainy photos. The Castalia Trout Club was equally opaque. They still held title; paid taxes, but had no clubhouse, membership or known activities.

For me the net was a definite red flag, warning of trouble ahead. To Frank it was a glitch to be brushed aside. Buying the sub had already blown his profit margin. This was no longer about money. It was about honor and Jim's body.

The next day we launched the sub with Frank and me aboard. It had two seats in a watertight cockpit, with an escape hatch for emergencies. I found the hatch and the scuba gear crammed in beside us less than comforting.

"Afraid of getting wet, Professor?" Frank teased, as we motored out to the center of the pond and opened the ballast tanks.

"Just of dying—soggy or not," I mumbled, as murky water swallowed us up.

The water had cleared somewhat since cleanup began. With the sub's lighting engaged we could just make out the trash ring and the dark hole at its center. Once through that hole the water became darker as daylight diminished. Frank closed all valves and steered us toward the outer edges. The walls of the hole were limestone with little growth attached. Above us we made out the braided remains of the net and its stanchions into solid rock. Spiraling downward, the hole's circumference increased. Much like Doctor Who's Tardis, this Blue Hole was bigger on the inside.

"Enough with the guided tour," Frank said. "Let's find Jim." He reopened the ballast valves and we sank like a mechanical stone. "Keep an eye on the gauges and let me know before we reach five hundred feet or use up our battery charge." he ordered—as if I had any damn practice monitoring either.

Webb's "underground spring" idea proved doubtful as we sank into a cavern vast enough for a major river. Luckily there was no real current to drag us away from our exit above. Luckier still, the crane's wreckage appeared directly below us.

"We're approaching three hundred feet," I warned. "And Frank, there's no damn way I'm getting out to snag Jim's body."

"Calm down, I've got two arms with claws I can manipulate from in here. How much power is left?" he said, closing all valves and steering us ever closer. Our battery was not yet an issue; but the crane, partially crushed and entangled in its own steel cables was. If Frank weren't careful, we might puncture our cockpit or become ensnared in the wreckage with scuba gear our only hope of escape.

"There's the cab," I said, pointing Frank toward our primary goal.

"Cab door's open, let's see if I can steer close enough to look inside." It took several passes and some ominous scraping of sub on cables before our lights pierced the crumpled interior. Jim's chair was empty, his seat belt open and that was all.

"He got out, he made it!" Frank shouted. "Where is

he now?"

"Jim drowned, Frank. Either down here or on the way up—probably trapped under the trash ring." Frank took a moment to accept this. Our task had never been to save Jim, but simply to find his body. We decided to search the bottom, still having sufficient battery power and spiraling out around the crane in widening circles. We found nothing of importance until skimming along one cavern wall.

"What the hell is that?" Frank said. "Wait, I see a body—no, I see bodies!" Indeed, there were bodies; perhaps hundreds of them stuck into rows of niches carved in the limestone. Squat, little beings with large skulls, sharp teeth and huge, empty eye sockets—all long dead, all bound in ritual postures like frogs on lily pads.

"Oh my God," Frank said, guiding our sub past row upon row. "What the hell is this, Professor? Please tell me you're seeing this cause I'm flipping out!"

"It's real alright," I said. "Maybe some kind of temple or mausoleum for the dead. Look, there are carvings, names or words maybe under each niche. Stop the sub, I've got to take some pictures."

"But whose dead," Frank whined. "These are not people—not people like us."

"I think they may be the net builders—all except for him." I said, pointing to Jim's lifeless body, bound like the others, at rest in a prominent upper niche.

* * *

It was difficult to calm Frank down. He was ready for

adventure, but not for this. I've crawled into tombs before, touched the dead, stared into the maw of the unknown. It's shameful to recall, but I had to slap him, force him to focus on recovering Jim's body and remaining silent on our return.

Topside, Jim's body drew all attention, allowing Frank a hero's spotlight. I drew back, planing how to document our find, take more photos, collect DNA. But my absence was noted. Mr. Webb stood ashore watching only me, his face twisted into a knowing, cynical grin. *What could be better to resurrect this faded, tourist trap*, I realized, t*han a sudden death, a daring recovery, and an ancient mystery?*

The Corporation sprang their trap quickly. They shut down the worksite, forbid more submarine trips below and declared any and all archeological finds to be the private property of Lakeline Corporation and The Castalia Trout Club.

I fought for scientific access through the media, raged against removal of any remains beyond the necessity of recovering Jim's body. Frank paid for lawyers and Cleveland State petitioned the Governor for historic preservation. But Lakeline had the big, political bucks and decided to replace the copper net with a new, stainless-steel version in the interest of "public safety."

I was beaten, but Frank was not. His company was still building the site, his sub was still in the water. Further exploration was possible before the net went in.

"You're insane," I said, one night in my car as we reconnoitered Lakeline's security measures. "They'll arrest you when you come back up."

"Who says I'm coming back up—this way?" He said. "This cavern must go somewhere. The Frogies got in to tie Jim's body up—while we were still working above. There has to be another way in and out."

"How will you find it?"

"We'll find it together," he said. "We'll sneak in every night, map the cavern and be back before dawn, until they finish the net—and I can stall that for weeks!"

"But I'm not going," I said.

"Why the hell not?"

"Because I'm not *foolishly brave*," I said. There was a long silence before Frank slapped me on the shoulder and got out of my car. Maybe he repaid the slap I gave him in the sub. Maybe he was saying goodbye, before sneaking off to new adventure.

"Okay old man," he said. "But you know what they say—no guts, no glory."

The current CRS (Carpathian Relief Society),
headquarters sat atop Cedar Hill, fronting Harcourt
Drive. It was a neo-gothic pile, ominous in the
Winter, but mostly hidden once leaf cover grew out.

Marginal

The annoying slivers of sunlight piercing the thread-bare covering overhead reluctantly awakened Renfield. He loathed abandoning his death-like sleep, but shit needed to get done—today was a feast day. Slowly unwrapping his dark cocoon of overcoat he opened his sunken eyes and strained to identify his location.

A flapping green plastic tarp above, a damp plaid blanket atop a spongy mat of discarded clothing below, and the raw stink of the Cuyahoga wafting through a dense surrounding thicket were all he had to go on. *Oh yes,* he remembered. *Irish Town Bend, West Bank of the Flats, south of the Main Avenue Bridge.* It was a sizable colony as these forgotten places go. Two-dozen makeshift tents were hidden amid the tangled overgrowth on both sides of the abandoned Old River Road. This was the White faction—hillbillies, PTSD vets, addicts, alkies, burnouts and a wide variety of mental defectives. Their Black and Hispanic doppelgangers were camped farther north under the looming hulk of the bridge. *"And neither the twain shall eat,"* he mused to himself. All were lost flotsam and jetsam of the early 21st century, washed up on the shoals of this dying city—Renfield's chosen people.

He slowly rolled himself downhill, out of the open side

of the meager shelter, thereby exposing the scant remains of his evening meal. A few broken Oreos littered the bottom of their torn plastic wrapper. "Sugar rush for breakfast," he murmured. "Who needs a damned Star-Bucks?" After downing the last stale crumbs like a drunk draining a whisky bottle, the wrapper was discarded haphazardly to join the carpeting of trash underfoot. Renfield then arose, painfully unfolding his gaunt black-clad form like some spectral, praying mantis disguised as a human being.

Being late morning, there was already some quarrel brewing in the no-man's-land between camps. "No rest for the wicked," he muttered under his pungent breath, and stalked purposely toward the contending parties.

"What's your problem, my son?" he croaked at the huge, tattoo-covered, sideshow freak of a man known as "Scorch" for his incendiary tendencies.

"This fat, little Mama-sita thinks she can squat with us, Parson!" Scorch howled, while he and a ragged pack of lesser toughs milled around facing off against one feisty latina and her terrified daughter.

"Well, can't she?" Renfield growled as he pushed through the crowd to stand chest to chest with the apparent alpha-dog leading them, meeting him blood-shot eye to eye.

"You know the rules," Scorch said, followed by a chorus of supportive grunts and yelps from his surrounding pack of indignant strays.

"Your rules or God's?" Renfield asked, distributing a paralyzing steely gaze at all involved.

"Jesus Christ, Parson." Scorch whined, as if the burden of civilized behavior was far too much to expect of himself and his fellow degenerates.

"Yes exactly, Jesus Christ would want to know," Renfield purred while advancing to interrogate the mother and child. "Why these two wandering innocents come seeking our generous protection."

"Them damn ped-oh-files under the bridge won't leave my Anita alone, Father," the woman said, taking Renfield's hand and kissing his dirty fingers as if she expected to discover a Papal ring.

Scorch and his minions roared with laughter at the notion their resident guttersnipe Pastor was any sort of celibate priest. In truth they had no idea what-so-ever about his credentials, but couldn't imagine they originated farther afield than the most disreputable regions of the lower Bible Belt.

Renfield sneered at the surrounding hilarity then carefully reached inside his soiled, black turtleneck and drew out a small golden crucifix on a delicate chain. The crowd went stone silent as he hung it visibly around his neck.

Of course the cross and chain were cheap gold plate, available at any jewelry counter or second hand store for peanuts. They no more defined his denomination than did his black clothes and casual acquaintance with Bible verse. Even an actual rosary would have proved nothing to knowledgeable believers. But for this herd of semi-heathen self-deluders, they both sanctified and mystified his standing beyond definition or censure.

"There's no room for her!" Scorch rallied, unwilling to easily surrender prejudice to piety.

"No room at the inn?" Renfield tisk-tisked, as he guided his new chattel through the loosening knot of deflated malcontents. "Such a tired, old answer for a deserving mother and child, don't you think? They can stay where I slept, for the time being."

"That's the Pollock's tent." Scorch barked at the backs of the triumphant trinity of mother, child, and holy father.

"And has anyone seen our Polish brother lately?" The supposed cleric mused without breaking his measured stride.

"No, but . . ."

"Then where's the damned harm?" Renfield tossed back over his hunched shoulder, knowing full well the poor Pollock's whereabouts and the non-existent odds of his return. "Shouldn't you boys be heading up to St. Malachi's? You'll be late for the free lunch."

The River Road camp's motley population drained out quickly—joining the daily migration uphill to the sad oasis of the church's soup kitchen. Renfield led his newly rescued dependents to their temporary sanctuary and commenced his usual instruction and grooming.

"You can stay here as long as necessary," he explained to the grateful mother. "No one will bother you while I'm in the neighborhood. But don't let dear little Anita out of your sight. This crowd is no different or better than those under the bridge—especially at night or back in these woods."

"Then how can I protect her?" the mother cried. "When you're not here with us, Father?"

"You must have faith, my child. It is not my protection

that matters, only his." Renfield raised two boney fingers and shook them at the empty sky. He was always amazed at the potency of such meaningless words and gestures. It was no wonder the good book called them sheep.

"Meanwhile give me your full names and as much information as you can possibly provide. There are government and charity programs—food stamps, housing vouchers, and income credits you might qualify for, and I'll make sure to sign you up. You'll see, I handle these formalities for all the homeless folks in town."

For a small percentage of any benefits of course, Renfield ruminated, as a detailed asset plan came together in his mind. They were probably not citizens, so wouldn't add to his lucrative absentee-voter portfolio. He could funnel the mother into a complicit temp agency as an under-the-table domestic. She wasn't attractive enough to work the streets. Realistically their major worth was little Anita, and at her apparent age (ten to thirteen years), she was a potential gold mine.

"There is a special private shelter I know of—they only accept mothers and children *(of a certain tender age),*" he added mentally. "Would you allow me to contact them about you?"

"Yes Father, bless you," the mother said, chocking back real tears of misplaced gratitude—which might have softened Renfield's stone of a heart, if he weren't already dead certain everyone must carry their own cross eventually.

*   *   *

Renfield lugged his plate of beans, hash browns, and half-eaten sandwich from table to table in the church's basement dining room. He was seeking out newcomers, gathering names, and forging useful dependency. This enhanced his always-precarious reputation and helped build his flock. His was a volume business, as the wretched homeless owned precious little to feed off of, and were prone to wander or even disappear entirely. It paid to keep ahead of the inevitable attrition, and so he "pressed the flesh" at every opportunity.

Billy Dog-breath rushed in and accosted him right there in the midst of a promising recruitment. Renfield made apologies and lured Billy away to a secluded hallway by sharing his sandwich. Whatever the odiferous Dog-breath had come to barter was best kept secret between them.

Well, what is it, Billy?" Renfield whispered. "You've never strayed this far from the tracks before."

"I knows, I'm sorry," slobbered the dirt-incrusted human mongrel stuffing his toothless face with Renfield's leftovers. "But we ain't seen youse in a long while Doc, and Maggie—she's doin' poorly."

Despite the grave implications, this was not unwelcome news. Billy hailed from another bleak, homeless squat near Tremont, beside railroad tracks servicing the steel mills. Maggie was his long-suffering companion. Probably no more than 40-ish, they had seen appalling years and she was now terminally ill. Renfield did what he could for her, which was little enough, given his medical training was every bit as sparse as his spiritual instruction. Allowing himself to be called "Doc" was about the extent of it.

"How poorly would you say?" Renfield asked, given the woman had already hovered just outside death's door long enough to require patio furniture.

"Bad Doc, real bad. So bad I hiked clean over here and near tore up these shoes." Billy claimed, lifting a foot barely attired in the remnants of sneaker and sock. "She may be done gone already."

"Never fear," Renfield said. "We'll go to her immediately. Finish up this . . . slop for me won't you? I'll pray for Maggie on our way to the car." The car was a nineteen sixty-four Econoline van—rusted out, with cracked windshield, and bald tires. It was a classic piece-of-shit, but the engine and brakes were reliable and it fit Renfield's no-budget profile perfectly when stashed among welfare-tenant transportation in CMHA's parking lot along nearby West Twenty-fifth Street. Once aboard, Billy finished topping up his pie hole and began fishing through piles of cast-off clothing for suitable replacement footwear while Renfield drove.

Renfield knew the exact location of every homeless camp in Cuyahoga County and was constantly scouting out more. He was the unofficial gondolier of drainage swamps, shepherd of brown fields, and concierge of abandoned buildings. While Dog-breath was reliably occupied, and under cover of a statically enhanced AM radio Bible station, Renfield fished out a hidden burner-phone from under the dashboard.

"Hello, I'd like to make a donation," Renfield whispered into the phone.

"Time of death," a bored voice replied.

"Any minute now," Renfield guessed.

"Is this you, Father Scarecrow?"

"Who else, my son?"

"You'd be surprised, Father. Shit's been crazy lately."

"Wanna bet?" Renfield hissed.

"Yeah, you seen it all I guess. Honk once and we'll let you in, but it better be natural—no blunt-force trauma, all right? We ain't covering for nobody."

"The Lord taketh and I hauleth away, my son."

"Amen to that," the voice said. "How long you think?"

"Half an hour maybe . . ."

"Golden hour's the limit, Father—unless they're iced down. After that they're just meat."

"I know," Renfield said shutting off the phone and pressing the gas pedal.

* * *

The Tremont squat was a study in violent contrasts, not so much an encampment as an assemblage of improvised huts cobbled together from shipping pallets and construction debris. It occupied the always-tenuous border between the aging industrial nightmare of chemical plants, steel mills, and train-yards and a gentrifying metrosexual paradise swiftly devouring ethnic neighborhoods that used to provide workers for those very industries between the world wars.

Its discarded denizens like Dog-breath and Maggie absorbed the toxic stench and poisons of rapacious capitalism while dinning out of elite dumpsters behind fine restaurants and trendy brewpubs. They were not welcome but routinely vilified and ejected from both environments. Plant guards and neighborhood police tag-teamed their oppression and the local councilman bulldozed their meager outpost on a semi-annual basis—only to allow its resurrection once his benign neglect focused elsewhere.

Maggie had not been actively engaged in this struggle for subsistence for a while now, although in her day she was a legendary hellcat. She'd been pallet-bound for months in the final throngs of some exotic lung-rot probably not seen since medieval serfdom. The Local free clinic did not make house calls and her aggressively hostile and abusive gun-moll personality was counter-productive everywhere else.

But she wasn't bullying or cussing-out anybody when Renfield and Billy arrived. Her outlaw swagger was long dead and the minimal whisper of shallow breath her lungs could still produce was now insufficient for words or survival. Billy never had worn the pants in this household, but his slavish dependency was even more abject now that her orders and oaths ceased entirely.

Renfield listened closely, his ear against her withered lips and his fingers on her emaciated wrist searching for some vestige of pulse. Twenty Years ago Maggie must have enjoyed a wild sort of beauty when she and Billy were some Appalachian version of Bonnie and Clyde. Now they were both rotting husks of misspent youth.

"Well," Renfield decided. "She isn't gone yet, but we need to get her into the van immediately."

"Ain't there no ambulance or such?" Dog-breath protested.

"How in God's name could you pay for that?" Renfield snapped back. "Do you and the Pirate Queen here have a liquor store heist in mind—a treasure chest of loot stashed in a culvert somewhere?"

"Well no, but ain't we a charity case, Doc?"

"Yes indeed, you are the very definition of destitute, but I'm all the social work she'll ever get—me and you Billy, that's it. Now grab two corners of the blanket she's laying on and I'll get the other two. Let's pray it holds together long enough to drag her out of here."

Prayer is answered . . . occasionally, at least it was in this case. Quigley Road ran right alongside the tracks so the van wasn't much more than a weedy drainage ditch away. Billy had always been the muscle of this delinquent duo and Renfield still commanded a surprising force of will animating his otherwise near-skeletal frame. They gingerly rolled her onto a bed of the cast-off clothing inside the van. Renfield slid the side cargo door closed and jumped into the driver's seat.

"Wait," cried Billy. "Can't I go with her, Doc?"

"Of course you can," Renfield said through the open driver's side door as he cranked the engine into a reluctant roar. "But should you? Ask yourself Billy; do I want to read and fill out all that difficult paper work; answer all those personal questions; provide all those identification papers to the authorities?"

"Well no, Maggie wouldn't like . . ." Billy hesitated, remembering the lifelong wrath of his stricken paramour toward all authority.

"I didn't think so," Renfield said. "You stay put here. I'll be back with news as soon as possible." Then he slammed the driver's door and sped away, leaving Dog-breath to contemplate his new depth of privation alone.

* * *

Outside the nondescript warehouse on the periphery of University circle, Renfield stopped the van under the harsh glare of security lights. He looked back at the figure lying in the back and tried to discern if she was still breathing.

"Well old girl, this is the end of the line, any last words or obscene gestures?" There was no visible response so he reached down for a soiled throw pillow that he kept below his seat. "Please forgive me for this," he said to nobody in particular. "We wouldn't want any nasty surprises for you, me, or the doctors would we?" Then Renfield glanced toward the conventional directions of Heaven and Hell saying, "I assume you knew she was coming. I leave it up to you to decide where she belongs."

Renfield bent over and worked his way awkwardly through the gap between the front seats. He knelt beside Maggie's body and placed the pillow gently but firmly on her unresponsive face. He held it there for some time. There was no hint of its necessity, which he appreciated, as his conscience was wretched enough already.

Back in the driver's seat he put the pillow away, drove up to the steel garage doors, and honked the horn once.

* * *

Inside the waiting room there were exactly six molded, plastic chairs and one coffee table. No posters hung on the beige walls, no drinking fountain working or not, no bathroom male or female, and two piles of old magazines (Sports illustrated and Popular Mechanics), that appeared virtually untouched. All across one wall of the room was a built-in Formica counter manned by two burley male receptionists behind sliding glass panels, who doubled as orderlies to unload bodies.

There was no obvious hint of hospital except for the clean ceramic flooring that smelled of disinfectant. Otherwise Renfield could have been waiting for an oil change and lube job. There was one unlocked metal door into the garage where the van waited and one locked metal door into the probable dissection room where the faint whir of bone saw and gurgle of fluid pump could occasionally be heard.

Renfield was nervous. It was after three in the afternoon. He had guests to round up and prep work to attend to before nightfall. Luckily it was summer and the Sun would not completely disappear until after nine p.m. And of course, he was feeling nauseous and a little shaky, which was normal on a feast day. Once per moon cycle was all that was necessary, but not all that could be desired.

Tomorrow he would feel buoyant and renewed, ready to take on the world. That was the hook that held him. That was the fix to die for. Soon afterward he'd feel like a helium balloon with a slow leak. Vitality hissing out of him from day to day until all he would feel was empty— like now—floating inches above the floor, depleted and desperate.

He wondered if the elders felt the same, if they were as dependent on him as he was on them? It was an interesting idea, but not one he dared to trust. The elders were strong, had always been strong, and he was weak. He was their pet, their toy mouse, an insect they might as well crush underfoot.

The doctor on duty entered from the locked room. He carried a black plastic bag and his white lab coat was stained like a butcher at the West Side Market. He was young, sounded foreign, and might have been an intern. Certainly no surgeon of standing would be caught harvesting organs on the down low.

"Her belongings and clothing," he said handing over the bag. Are you aware she carried a knife strapped to a leg under her robe? No underwear, just a knife."

"No," Renfield admitted. "But she was a rough and ready girl, I guess."

"I am believing this, it appeared she resided out of doors," he said. "She was very, very fresh, so this was excellent, but you know . . . very much diseased."

"What did she have?"

"What didn't she have?" he said making a face of exaggerated surprise. "Cancer, heart disease, double pneumonia, maybe tuberculosis, possibly syphilis—you can be naming it."

"What killed her?" Renfield asked, hoping it wasn't asphyxiation.

"Who is knowing," he sighed. "Her lungs and heart, no good. Better news, two excellent eyes, two kidneys, and one liver. So . . . here is four hundred fifty dollars cash," he finished, offering Renfield a small stack of used bills.

"No medical school cadaver fee?" Renfield asked before accepting payment.

"Schools today must be very, very careful. They require signed permission and over much documentation. This is not being England in the eighteen fifties, sir."

To be clear, we would not be dealing with you, if not for impossible transplant backlogs. Everybody is saying—organ transplant yes, organ donation no."

"How about grave robbers?" Renfield joked, taking his cash.

"Oh good heavens no! We do not employ body snatchers here, sir. No offense implied, you understand."

"None taken." Renfield said, and walked out the door.

* * *

Renfield stood in front of a blazing trashcan near where Doan Brook dumped into the lake. This old landfill sight was now a bird sanctuary. No homeless camps were allowed, but construction companies still staged their equipment and trash there when working on the shoreway. He was burning Maggie's clothes, belongings, and anything else from the van that might have been infected. The knife was at the bottom of the lake as far out has he could heave it. There was no telling what it had been used for, and Renfield had zero interest in being associated with the misdeeds of others. His own were more than sufficient.

That impulse proved clairvoyant when a squad car

pulled up behind the van and disgorged what passed for the city's finest, officers Cain and Fagan. "You catch a chill, Padre?" Cain sneered. "Cause it must be at least seventy-five out here."

"Just disposing of some trash, officers," Renfield answered.

"That's funny," Fagan added. "Cause trash is kind of your specialty, isn't it? Human trash that is." Officer Cain then grabbed his nightstick and placed its business end against Renfield's chest, pushing him back against the van. Fagan began using his own cudgel to stir the van's interior in search of unknown evidence.

"I wouldn't express it that way, but yes," Renfield admitted. "You could say I minister to the unwanted."

"Word is you made a donation of something unwanted less than an hour ago," Cain said. "Is that true, Parson?"

"I normally receive donations, not make them. Is there something I could help you gentlemen find?"

"An extra two hundred dollars would be nice," Fagan said, slamming his stick against the van floor for emphasis. "Two hundred each."

I don't carry nearly that much," Renfield pleaded. "And I need everything I have to pay for an . . . event tonight, an important charity event, you understand."

"We know what the Clinic pays, Father friggin' Nightmare!" Cain yelled in his ear. "You just dumped a body from one of your beggar-farms, and that's one less for us to pick up and cash in. Now, we don't give a rat's ass if you enjoy doing the heavy lifting. Be our damned guest, you old ghoul—but we need a cut or we're shutting down your whole stinking operation."

"My *operation* is a ministry to the poorest of the poor . . . Renfield claimed as strongly as dubious circumstances allowed. "Whatever meager funds I receive are spent on helping them." In response, Cain crammed his nightstick up under the crucifix still hanging around the Renfield's neck and ripped it away. The chain broke, flinging the tiny cross to the ground.

"What *ministry* faggot?" Fagan howled, slamming Renfield against the van. "You child molester, you medical hack, and whatever other frauds you pretend to practice!" Cain landed a vicious club blow across Renfield's face sending him to his knees where both cops continued to kick and beat him onto the ground.

"You got a real church somewhere old man?" F agan taunted as he dragged the bleeding figure back up to face him. "You even ordained or licensed for any of the damned shit you do?"

"I am . . . SELF-ORDAINED!" Renfield roared. "I am LICENSED by the LORD!"

"Well, that explains it," a voice said calmly but distinctly from a distance.

Renfield and the two officers froze, looking toward a beefy older man in a suit and crumpled hat approaching from an unmarked police car.

"You officers get back to your beat now. I'll handle the Reverend from here," The detective said, lighting a cigarette while Cain and Fagan dropped Renfield back to the ground and tried to resume some appearance of professionalism.

"We were just . . ." Cain stammered.

"I know what you were doing. Now beat it," the detective said. After the squad car left, the detective helped Renfield up to a sitting position on the floor of the open van. "Rough day, Reverend?" he asked.

"You could say that," Renfield answered before licking the blood from his lips and fingers with more relish than the detective thought necessary.

"Look, I can't do anything official, because what you and the officers were . . . discussing is a taboo-subject between City Hall and the Clinic, understand?"

"Completely," Renfield said.

"I can guarantee it won't happen again, if you'll help us thin your flock . . . weed out a few rotten apples, and such."

"I don't know . . ." Renfield said, weighing compromise against compassion.

"Otherwise, I'll have to see your license, check your registration, run the plates, see about insurance—and I know you got an . . . event to deal with, right?"

"Jesus Christ, how long were you listening before you stopped them?"

"Just long enough."

*   *   *

The detective proved a godsend. He flashed Renfield a stack of mug shots—all wanted felons suspected of laying low in Cleveland. Two stood out. Billy Dog-breath wasn't his real name but the lack of teeth matched. Renfield felt Billy would be better off in jail. He wouldn't be lonely, and Renfield could crash at Billy's shack without sharing the sad news of his true love's passing. As for Maggie's mug shot, Renfield honestly reported her missing.

Before leaving, the detective picked up Renfield's busted chain and crucifix. "Here, Padre," he said tossing them back. "You might still need these."

From that moment on, Renfield had to marshal all his remaining energy toward the feast. He had less than four hours before his elders expected satisfaction and disappointing them was not an option. First he had to buy groceries and gather his chosen guests from all over Cleveland's homeless community, then he must transport everything to society headquarters and prepare the meal. Luckily his elders never dinned until after dark, so daylight savings time was a lifesaver this time of year.

He practically ran through Dave's Supermarket pushing and pulling two shopping carts. Usually he'd do Heinen's or Whole Foods, but now he had no time for up-scale. Quality was mostly in the presentation anyway and his elders preferred candlelight. The homeless probably couldn't tell gourmet from garbage and everyone would be drinking heavily.

Renfield selected his guests by a sort of reverse lottery. The worst losers sunk to the top of his list. The most lonely, least functional, and worst behaved all qualified, but least friendly or most disliked counted double. He never took more than one from each encampment and encouraged secrecy to avoid envy and retribution. They usually played along, universal greed and vanity being reliable vices. Five quests were optimal, Renfield made it six, and his elders craved variety.

* * *

Current CRS (Carpathian Relief Society), headquarters
sat atop Cedar Hill fronting Harcourt Drive. It was an old
neo-gothic pile, ominous in Winter but hidden once leaf
cover grew out. Renfield had arranged it, as he arranged
all their locations since fleeing Austro-Hungary in 1850.
Berlin, Paris, London, New York—the Society got around.
Hopefully their recent change to a smaller city and less
aggressive resource management would keep them in the
Cleveland area for the foreseeable future.

The two male and three female guests were suitably
impressed upon arrival. They failed to take notice of Renfield unlocking the front door or the lack of receptionist or
staff. They seemed to like having the place to themselves.

Renfield got everybody to help ferry groceries to the
kitchen and uncorked a bottle of wine to lighten the mood
in the echoing hallways and empty rooms. No one noticed
he did not partake of that bottle, but instead drank deeply
from a dusty unlabeled bottle left loosely-corked in the
kitchen. His was a dark red vintage, almost viscous in
texture, which seemed to invigorate him greatly.

In this elevated mood Renfield took his guests on tour,
up the wide staircase into a grand dinning room with a
huge table surrounded by chairs. The table was already
set with fine china, silverware, and three candelabra down
the center.

He threw open heavy drapes exposing arched windows—a veritable palace except for its somber hues and dark carpets, more funeral parlor than fairytale ballroom. Then Renfield showed them two large separate bathrooms marked for men and women complete with showers and dressing rooms lined with racks of clean suits and dresses fit for a night at the opera. "Ladies and gentlemen," he said. "Please take some time to spruce yourselves up and try on any garments you please, while I do all the cooking. Our hosts wish this to be the best party of your lives!"

It took time for the guests to warm to such luxuries, having lived unwashed in rags for years. As Renfield chopped vegetables, he began to hear running water, smell fragrances, and imagine joy over clean, fluffy towels. He felt a strange sensation. *Was that a smile reflected on this saucepan? My smile?* Yes, but the length of his yellowed incisors made him flinch away. *No mirrors,* he thought. *No mirrors!* By the time the meat went in, he overheard chatter about hemlines, decisions over flats or heels, and the struggle with a Windsor knot.

Renfield brought out another bottle and witnessed rehabilitated swains and sweethearts deciding where to sit and who to flirt with. They weren't country club ready, but would no longer repel his elders—which was the point. It was difficult to bend their expectations. The nightly thrill of young blood was addictive. Only constant fear of discovery, sunlight, and sharp objects brought eventual acquiescence. Real death was permanent no matter how long you dodged it.

* * *

Finally all was ready. Even Renfield cleaned up in the scullery sink (which had no mirror), and changed into a clean copy of what he wore previously. Candles were lit and food came out. Everyone helped, wine flowed, it was a party. Renfield made everyone spread out to accommodate their hosts. He promised a lavish desert upon their arrival, but hadn't made one. The real feasting wouldn't last that long.

As the Sun went down, candle flames glowed brighter. Shadows advanced from the surrounding walls and the full moon shone through arched windows. Conversation waned and the nocturnal creaks and groans of the old house intruded. Renfield finished the last dregs of his special vintage and excused himself to use the bathroom. It was time for him to leave. He dared not look back.

* * *

On his way down the stairs Renfield saw them, materializing up from the cellar like gathering fog. Dressed in antique finery they floated soundlessly up the stairs passing by on their way to the dinning room. He bowed to them and they acknowledged his service with haughty smiles of sharp white teeth.

Locking the front door as he left, Renfield reached into his pocket and drew forth the tiny crucifix in his hand. It glowed brightly in the moonlight, but only felt slightly warm to the touch. It didn't burn him or force him to look away. This was how Renfield knew, how he gauged his precarious position. He was not a Saint, far from it. But he was no God-Damned Vampire either. . .

It took a while to chop a hole
big enough to pull Fritz out, but
when the three men did—they
wished to God they hadn't.

Below Freezing

Henri deGraf descended, in a tenuous, convoluted line, from French fur trappers—the first europeans to explore and exploit Lake Erie. He captained a charter boat in nice weather and drove a snow plow when nature got brutal. He was more that old enough to start a family, but the holiday atmosphere of the west basin of Lake Erie distracted him, and Henri remained single.

He also had a certain affinity for "The White World" as he called it. Not the terrestrial latitudes dominated by fellow caucasians, but with the domain of frozen water, the vast areas periodically or permanently buried under ice and snow. Realms possessed, silenced and stilled by the power of temperature itself. A frigid, white grip that strangled the botanical world into slumber, except for lonely pine and fir trees still standing green and defiant.

His own breath, indicative of life and activity blew out visibly before him, turning into mist and attaching itself to his facial hair as frosted, glistening icicles, proclaiming the threat of the transfixed—the frozen over the animate. Anybody, even Henri, could easily die out here.

Wouldn't that be something? He thought, as his snowmobile carried him further and further out over the ice towards the islands. *It wouldn't take all that much—just a freak Northeaster blowing in from upstate New York, across still open water near Cleveland and laying down three feet of heavy snow on Sandusky Bay.* Henri wondered when the last time was somebody froze to death out there. Of course people did drown, fell through broken ice, floated ashore the next Spring. Folks died all the time on Lake Erie—Spring, Summer and Fall. All it took was heavy drinking and/or the lack of a life jacket, which he wasn't even wearing himself.

Not gonna happen to me, he thought. *This ice is a good foot thick if it's an inch.* Besides, he was nearly at his destination. A spattering of ice fishing shanties loomed in the distance. He was running way late from too much hard partying the night before. A half dozen snowmobiles were already out there. Thin wisps of smoke arose from a couple of sheds that sported heaters. *Pussies,* Henri thought. *These old guys should give up ice fishing if they can't handle the cold.*

Normally he would stop in at various shanties, say hello and share some "hair of the dog" with old friends. Russian vodka with Dimitri, plum brandy with the Polish brothers and rot-gut moonshine with Fritz, his father's aged buddy. Henri's Dad was long gone, but Fritz was eternal, like Old Man Winter itself.

But this morning Henri was unforgivably tardy, hung over and probably already far behind in the fishing derby that crowned every ice-angler's frosty day. Twenty bucks for the most fish per day and fifty for that season's prize catch—the largest Bass, Pike or giant Muskellunge, the true monster of Lake Erie. Instead he pulled up to his father's dilapidated wooden shanty, scraped frost off the small window, unlocked the door and dragged his gear inside.

The portable shanty was small, about five foot square and six foot high, mounted on two metal skids. It contained only a stool, tiny charcoal grill for cooking and a sixteen-inch wide hole augered out at the beginning of the season. The hole was iced over from last weekend, but Henri brought a hand axe to chop it open again. Inside it was cold as a witch's tit, but with the wind blocked and some vigorous chopping Henri's chill subsided and he settled into fishing as soon as the broken ice was scooped aside.

There was no casting involved and minimal reeling in so ice fishing was mostly contemplation and conversation—if you had a partner. Henri and his father did their best male bonding over that dark, wet hole, but now all questions and insights were for himself alone.

How do fish stand it? He wondered. Dark, wet, shut off from the sky above, breathing what would drown us whilst we thrive on what suffocates them. It must be cold and lonely down there. No wonder they swim up to what light seeps through this fatal hole. Then they get rewarded with a tasty, little snack—just before being yanked out by the hook, sliced open and fried to death in a pan. *Some life,* he thought to himself. *Some fucking, sad, little life.*

It wasn't long before two fat perch flopped themselves toward death on the icy, shanty floor beside him. *I'm not winning today's fish derby,* Henri thought. *Might as well gut these guys, fire up the grill and make lunch.* He cracked the roof vent open to dispel smoke and melted a handful of ice shards for instant coffee. He still had a baited line down, so when he caught a glimpse of something bone-white in the water,

Henri bent down to check it out.

That something was half submerged and lifeless, probably a dead carp floating belly up with the lake current—the millions of gallons flowing relentlessly under the ice from the upper lakes, toward the falls at Niagara and then on out to the North Atlantic.

"You got a long, long way to go, Buddy," he said, reaching into the frigid water to haul it out for identification. But he didn't lay hold of a fish, he felt a wrist and then a whole hand. "Jesus Fucking Christ!" He bellowed. "Somebody come and help, there's a body under here!"

Henri kicked his stool, charcoal grill and fishing rig out of the way and pulled with all his might. An arm and sopping wet sleeve came out of the depths, but he could not get the neck, head and shoulder through his limited opening in the ice.

"Dimitri, Fritz, anybody out there, come and help for Christ's sake!" There was a loud commotion outside the shanty and the two Polish brothers, Stash and Yuri burst through his door.

"Did you fall in?" Stash asked.

"What's your problem?" Yuri added. "All this yelling scares the fish away and we' re already late getting out here—but not half as late as you Frenchy."

"Somebody is drowning!" Henri shouted. "Help me get him out of this hole!"

"We'll have to use your axe. Keep hold of his coat till we move him around and get his head above water," Stash said, while all three men reached down to their shoulders in the freezing water muscling the body into position. When the head came up, yanked by it's long, white hair all three screamed in shock—nearly loosing their grip on the victim.

"Oh my God, it's Fritz!" Henri said, hallucinating for a moment his own father's dying continence on the corpse-white face of a beloved friend. Stash, a trained EMT ashore, held the old man's face as clear of the water as possible and tried to perform mouth to mouth resuscitation, but the mouth wouldn't open. Frigid rigor mortis had already set in.

"I'm sorry Henri, the old guy's already dead," Stash said, ordering his brother to go back out and check Fritz's shanty to see how this happened, while keeping Fritz's body from sinking. Henri used his ax to widen the ice hole enough to remove the body.

Yuri came back to report the entire ice floor under the old man's shanty had been ripped away, his stool and fishing gear bobbing in open water. It took a while to chop a hole big enough to pull Fritz out, but when the three men did—they wished to God they hadn't.

Fritz had no body below his navel. The tattered remains of his upper winter clothing dangled down amid a grotesque fringe of mangled flesh and intestines.

"What the hell could have done this?" Henri moaned.

"Maybe his heater exploded," Stash guessed, having seen some similar carnage from house fires and car wrecks.

"That's not all," Yuri added. "We're alone out here. All the other shanties are empty with their snowmobiles still parked outside. Whoever killed Fritz took everybody."

"Except us," Henri gulped. " Maybe the ice shifted into Canadian waters and the royal mounties think we're invading. Let's take Fritz's body and get-the-hell out of here.'"

Just then the sound of splintering wood came from outside. Henri opened his door just in time to see Dimitri's splintered shanty dragged under the ice through ever-widening fractures all around them. He knew it was impossible, but thought he saw scaly, serpentine coils or tentacles lifting sheets of ice, toppling shanties and dragging snowmobiles around on the heaving surface.

For a stunned moment Henri wondered if old Fritz had hooked something ancient and terrifying, pulled it up to claim that season's trophy—before being gutted and half eaten himself. But Fritz's body and improbable fate no longer mattered. Mortal danger now loomed for the Polish brothers and himself.

Henri lit out on his snowmobile followed by Stash and Yuri riding double on their own. The nearest shoreline was miles away and the wind had shifted against them, blowing waves of stinging ice crystals in their faces. Henri had no idea how they would describe what had happened to the authorities—he simply prayed they'd have the chance.

Behind them, whatever attacked the shanties was busting a crevice through the frozen surface ice like Godzilla coming for Tokyo. And to either side of this onrushing terror, man-sized, frog-like creatures on stolen snowmobiles fanned out to flank the humans' escape.

Nobody brings firearms to ice fish, but Henri wished he had at least retained his hand ax. He and the brothers should beat their pursuers to the shoreline. Enough snow had fallen to continue across the beach, but what would happen further ashore he could not imagine.

In the end he wouldn't have to. The offshore wind had shifted Erie's ice sheet eastward and strong currents flowing from the Maumee and Detroit Rivers did far worse, flooding the widening gap between the floating ice sheet and the shoreline. Henri and the Polish brothers had a sizable lead and could probably out maneuver the frog-ish posse that was undoubtably new to motorized transport . . . but nothing besides open, frigid water lay ahead and their pursuers seemed to know that.

Jake the dog catcher, parked his work van behind the red barn on Tinker's Creek Road to avoid unwanted scrutiny. He took off his official day-glow vest for similar reasons. It was a steep hike along the wooded hillside to the solitary Stone House perched high above Canal road, but his profession and destination were not strictly compatible.

Bad Breeds

Jake the dog catcher, parked his work van behind the red barn on Tinker's Creek Road to avoid unwanted scrutiny. He took off his official, day-glow vest for similar reasons and donned a green hoodie just in case. It was a steep hike along the wooded hillside to the solitary stone house perched high above Canal Road, but his profession and destination were not strictly compatible.

Approaching the rear of the house, Sybil's mongrels raised their hackles and bared teeth. Jake spoke the Latin warning she'd taught him, copied from the ruins of Pompeii, guaranteeing their silent obedience. Even so, their mistress was at the door before he made to knock.

"Do we have business?" she said, opening the weathered oak door just a crack. "You know what day this is?"

"I know," Jake answered, performing his practiced, nod of deference. "I'll be long gone before nightfall, Miss Arkham."

"See that you are." Then Sybil let him enter, secure the door behind them, and follow her long, black skirts into the ornate parlor. "Well?" she said, sitting on a carved mahogany rocker and cuddling Nightshade, the large, black cat who was her constant, indoor companion.

"I caught me a bad one this time, Miss Sybil—a real

monster."

"Aren't all the flea-bitten curs you capture, by definition, bad ones?" she teased.

"Oh, no. Most is just strays or runaways," Jake said. "A few has gone wild as it were, mated up with fox or coyote and formed packs. But them I mostly poison."

"Hmm . . . such a waste of quarry. I hope you don't lay poison around here."

"No Miss, I only does that outside Cuyahoga Valley National Park. Them park rangers get mad as hell 'bout unnatural death. They even gathers up the roadkills and sets them out for buzzards." Sybil had a good cackle imagining such squeamish behavior. She was fond of Jake, his rural manner and wary subservience. He amused her as a useful partner in crime.

"Tell us about this monster," she said, as if Nightshade also required consultation.

"Oh, he's a mean one, he is. Some sort of hound or mastiff, and big! Yow-wee, he must come near up to my waist standing still. Tear a man's throat out without ever gettin' airborne."

"Sounds like he belonged to the Baskervilles," Sybil joked.

"Don't rightly know who they was," Jake admitted. "But he's the very devil himself and a champion if I ever saw one."

"But is he intact?" She asked, as a worthy sire was vital to Sybil's peculiar interests.

"Hung like two green apples. The Dutchman says he could mount a mare if need be."

"Damn the Dutchman!" Sybil shouted, lurching off the rocker and sending Nightshade leaping to the floor. "Idiot bumpkin, I thought you had him!"

"I did Miss, but the Dutchman runs the pits and owns the current champion. Rules say he has first dibs on any new contender. You gotta cut a deal with Gunther to get ahold of him."

After kicking Jake out, Sybil had to prepare herself. She released two howling, captive strays from her basement dog pens and set them loose into the deep woods. ***"Run, you wild things!"*** she bellowed after them. ***"Taste the freedom of the forest while you can."*** Then she stripped herself, painting dark, Celtic runes all over her body. As the full moon rose and the blood boiled within her, she set out for the hunt, naked and barefoot in the chill of night.

* * *

The Dutchman, Gunther Van Der Welk was rogue Amish, a dangerous mix of rural piety and modern corruption. He and Sybil shared a tragic Rumspringa hookup during that traditional, Amish period of adolescent license, which had deeply scarred them both. He with guilt and thwarted desire—she with a damaged womb and lust for revenge. Sybil had aborted herself, with a crochet hook when only fifteen, just to spite him.

Gunther now maintained a proper Amish homestead, with a frumpy, blonde wife and six dull-witted children somewhere out in the farmlands beyond Middlefield. He supported them by operating a shadowy, illegal network of organized cruelty all over northeastern Ohio.

"To what do I owe this pleasure?" Gunther said, as Sybil arrived with Jake at a secluded sawmill crowded with pickup trucks and horse-drawn buggies, south of New Franklin, Ohio.

"To the devil we both do serve," Sybil said, as the German Shepherd she held by a sturdy leash snarled and snapped toward Gunther's nether regions. Gunther should have parried with holy scripture, but failed to recall any. Instead he attacked their mutual ally, Jake, the dog catcher.

"Told her about the hound did you? No honor among thieves, I guess."

"I don't rightly steal dogs," stammered Jake. "I catches them and takes my cut from the pound or a buyer. Since you ain't paid me yet, I guesses Miss Arkham is just another customer."

"Says her sniveling lap dog." Gunther barked.

"There was a time you desired that position," Sybil sneered through black lipstick that matched the leather outfit she wore from head to foot. "Now take us to the hound."

Gunther had his prize chained up in a separate shed from the saw-barn where the main events would take place. The moment they entered, the hound began howling and straining against its chains. Brutus, the German Shepard, tried to back out the door rather than face such menace, but Sybil was instantly smitten. Jake and Gunther stood back to watch her pay court.

The creature was all coal-black, a Great Dane mixed with a bit of Bull Mastiff. His bulging eyes were red-rimmed and his gaping, mouth slather soaked the wooden floor—marking the semi-circular range of his deadly jaws.

"He's beautiful," Sybil whispered, approaching as close as anyone dared.

"And with him being so dark, he'll look just like one of your family," Jake said. Sybil laughed at this, combing her free hand through her own long, raven tresses. It was true the Arkham clan had always presented a marked absence of light. They were a very old Massachusetts family that began their westward retreat from civilization shortly before the Salem witch trials—ending up in the Western Reserve several decades after the American revolution.

But now they were trapped within the Cuyahoga Valley National Park. Their venerable, stone farmhouse was still theirs as long as it was inhabited by blood relations, but forfeited to the Park Service if ever they sold it or died off.

This was the dagger hanging over Sybil. The Arkhams were a dying breed. Never a numerous clan, they were slow to marry and hard to multiply. They had a habit of dying mysteriously, never seeming to leave more than a single living thread to extend their bloodline.

Sybil's father, Magnus Arkham was no exception. He was run over during a full moon in the middle of Canal Road by a mysterious, speeding, pickup truck not using its headlights. Why old Magnus was buck naked at the time was considered highly mysterious as well.

Now there was only Sybil. While she was thought beautiful and highly desirable by all who gazed upon her—she was difficult to please and impossible to tame. Gunther had already found this out to his shame and anger, and Jake, just as smitten, was not up to the challenge.

Down on her knees now, eye to eye with the vicious hound, Sybil whispered to the beast. "I have special plans for you and me." At this, the hell hound quieted as if Sybil's azure gaze had cast a spell of expectation. The creature whimpered and licked its lips.

"I dare you to kiss him." Gunther taunted.

"Not quite yet," Sybil replied, "in public," before rising again to confront the Dutchman. "How much do you want for him?"

"I don't know yet," Gunther mused. "We'll see after today's matches."

"Good," she said, "I'll know what I can pay by then."

The Dutchman's matches were held roughly twice a month, timed to the waxing and waning of the moon. Locations were kept secret, randomized by season and spread out over the hinterlands around major cities and towns. There were also urban matches, but these were controlled by various ethnic drug gangs, often proved violent, and were therefore shunned by Gunther's yokel sportsmen. Women, like Sybil, were rarely participants anywhere.

Gunther's dog fighting pits were corrugated-metal livestock ponds available in various sizes at farm equipment suppliers. This sawmill accommodated a pit twenty feet in diameter with four- foot high walls. Instead of water it held four inches of sawdust, which the sawmill had in abundance, and which provided traction and soaked up blood.

The match was crowded, with a double row of farmers hugging the pit walls. Brutus was listed on the betting board in the first round, against a Rottweiler named Thor. Sybil paid the fifty-dollar fee and took up a prime location in the front row—being as much an attraction as her fighting dogs. Urban matches favored the appropriately-named Pit Bulls, but rural contests were more eclectic, seeing as how most farm animals were ultimately raised to be slaughtered anyhow.

Most dogs were thrown into the pit. Trained to be lethal and aggressive by nature, they would attack anything that moved. Sybil's dogs were more strategic. She chose wolfish breeds with long muzzles and sharp, prominent canines—teeth that delivered deep puncture wounds to bleed out an opponent's will to fight. Her dogs leapt into the pit on her command.

Dogs, like wolves, are primarily pack hunters. Individual conflicts were more about dominance and once an animal became tired or hurt they would "belly up" exposing their vitals to attack. This ended most matches—unless the victorious dog was trained to kill. Brutus was practiced in this restraint, but would go for the kill when necessary. This day Brutus won five rounds of matches, only killing once—a vicious Bull Terrier named Rex that chomped onto his rear leg and would not let go. Brutus snapped the Terrier's neck, but Sybil had to withdraw her dog from further competition so Jake could attend to the wounded leg.

Still the matches were lucrative. Vigorous side-betting against her animal had mounted, believing Brutus would tire and lose. There was pent-up desire to see a woman fail in such masculine spectacles. Sybil knew this, relished it, and profited greatly from such ignorance.

"I'm ready to deal," she told Gunther. "I'll give two hundred fifty dollars for the hound."

"I want a thousand," the Dutchman replied.

"One thousand for a dog that's not yours to begin with? That's too greedy, even for you!"

"He's not mine, yours or Jake's—but I promised Jake half, so he won't take your side."

"I only made five hundred today including the fifty I paid to enter."

"So you'll owe me five hundred. You can work it off— at say, one hundred a night?"

"Fuck you!" Sybil said, moving to attack him, but Gunther caught and held her hands.

"How old are you Sybil, nearly forty? You need a child, and I gave you the last one."

Sybil spat in his face, pulling away when he used his sleeves to wipe off. They began circling each other like rabid dogs. It was a grudge match both had nursed for many years.

"Tell you what," Gunther said. "We'll gamble on it— the hound against my champion bulldog, Grendel. If the hound wins, you get him for free. But if Grendel wins, I get your five hundred dollars and keep whatever's left of the damn hound!"

"The hound isn't trained to fight."

"God damn right!" Gunther cursed. "If you train that monster, he'll ruin my business. Nobody in their right mind would bet against you and that hell hound."

When the regular matches ended, Gunther announced a new event. The hound was wrestled into the pit and the Dutchman led in Grendel, his mammoth English Bulldog so armored with fat and muscle he was nearly impervious to normal bites. His mouth was as wide as a bear trap and his legs so short it was almost impossible to attack his vitals from below.

The two beasts bellowed at each other as if to win by volume alone. Grendel attacked first, rushing under the taller animal. The hound sprang away uncertain why it was being charged. It was like a match between a giraffe and a turtle—one leaping around the pit and the other scuttling back and forth in the sawdust. Grendel drew first blood chomping on a forepaw. But the hound finally realized his situation, and bit onto the bulldog's ear from above.

Sybil recognized both dogs' weaknesses, the bulldog's bulging eyes and the hound's dangling testicles, but could not shout instructions to the hound as she would with Brutus. Gunther yelled encouragements at Grendel, but the size difference frustrated his champion as it labored to chase the larger, more agile hound around and around the pit. As the match dragged on, Sybil could see the Dutchman's temper beginning to boil over.

After both animals tired, it became a stand off, long-clawed forepaws against iron jaws. A lucky jab to Grendel's eyes might decide victory, but the Dutchman couldn't tolerate losing. Instead, Gunther and Jake threw two more bulldogs into the pit. The hound was doomed. The fight became a three against one massacre. Sybil's hope was literally torn to shreds.

After a long, silent drive back to the Cuyahoga valley in his van, Jake said, "You know I was only following Gunther's orders."

"If you knew anything about history you'd understand how fucking lame that sounds," Sybil growled, cradling her bandaged dog, Brutus in her lap on the passenger seat.

"Look Miss Sybil, Gunther's my bread n' butter," Jake whined. "Being county dog warden don't pay shit and I sure ain't gettin' rich being your hired man."

"If you were truly *my man* you'd profit greatly," Sybil said, angrily getting out of his van behind the red barn. Then her voice grew cold and echoed strangely in the woods behind her. **"I have power to bestow both favors and curses, Jake. But you have proved weak, ignorant and treacherous. So heed me now—if ever you come here again, my dogs will have you."**

* * *

After breaking with Jake and the Dutchman, Sybil had to rebuild her lifestyle. She focused on a circle of "wise" women in the area, and although she was known to all as a "night sister" they respected her lineage. This suburban coven had become mostly faith healers, fortune tellers and venders of crystals, essential oils and scented candles—pale echos of their ancient callings.

She quickly gathered a powerful, female triad (not unlike the "weird sisters" in Macbeth), with Hester, an elderly, serial widow know for marrying and burying husbands and Dominique, a young Voodoo priestess from Haiti.

Both of whom were "up to no good" as Sybil preferred.

Hester was an animal lover, a "cat lady" in millennial parlance, who worked at the old Cleveland Humane Society on Wiley Road in the gentrified Tremont neighborhood. Dominique ran a storefront on Kinsman Road, in a neighborhood avoided by whites. The love potions, good luck charms and zombie curses she brewed there were the least illegal of her many enterprises.

If Sybil needed dogs, she relied on Hester. If she needed to win cash with Brutus, she invoked Dominique's criminal contacts and the protection of her large, ex-con brother, Titus.

This new life cost Sybil dearly. Adoptions at the dog pound weren't free and the animals were spayed, neutered or required shots, which for Sybil's purposes were less than useless.

The urban dog fighting circuits were dangerous and even more costly. Sybil had to pay Titus a flat fee and a percentage of her winnings for transportation and armed safety, lest she find herself up for auction in these hyper-masculine, substance-infused and criminal environments.

Of course, her most existential need remained—not that many unworthy suitors refrained from presenting themselves. As hateful and lacking as Gunther and Jake had been, they at least understood her. The suits, fops and thugs that sniffed around her now turned her stomach.

She searched in vain through numerous animal shelters for the likes of the murdered hound that had offered a desperate, arcane solution. Then Hester found her another prospect.

"Why is this boy in a cage?" Sybil said, when brought to the shelter early one morning.

"Arturo begs to be. It makes him feel safer," Hester said. "I lock him in every night."

"Where are his clothes?" said Sybil, averting her eyes from his naked, sleeping form.

"Outside the cage. He fears he'll tear them up while dreaming, and they're all he owns."

"And you approve of this . . . bizarre situation?"

"How else will an old gal like me get to ogle young, bare, man butt?" Hester joked.

Arturo was sent to Cleveland in a bus full of migrants from Texas. Governor Abbot of Texas wanted northern cities like Cleveland to share his illegal immigrant load. Arturo's small size, gaunt condition and lack of documents made his age uncertain, and minors were typically released to sponsors. He was used to working with animals, so he was either going to work for the Humane Society or the Zoo. Hester was happy for the help and let him live for free on site.

Sybil spent many days talking with Arturo as he went about his duties at the shelter. Although he knew little English, Sybil had studied Spanish in high school and managed to learn something about his former life and how he came to the United States. He had spent most of his life in dire poverty, driven out of his home village and living like a hermit in the Copper Canyon wilderness of Northern Mexico. She was especially intrigued when he admitted the reason for this partially, self-inflicted plight and his desire to hide among strangers up north.

"Yo soy maldito," he admitted, which meant he believed himself accursed. Curses were something Sybil understood intimately, and his need to be caged at night implied even more.

"I'll take him," Sybil decided. "How much do you want?"

"Lordy," Hester clucked. "He's not for sale, he just works here! You can be his sponsor."

* * *

Gunther and Jake were drinking and smoking behind a barn in Lake County after their latest event. The dog matches had been poorly attended since a certain star attraction refused to show. They talked of drafting somebody's wife or girlfriend to provide the missing sex appeal, but even rural, party girls weren't keen on watching pets die.

"You know," Jake said, "Sybil's got a new guy, a Mexcan who works at the dog pound."

"Since when?" Gunther grunted.

"About two months ago. They're shacked up in her stone house right now. I heard it from Hester, the old woman what runs the animal shelter and takes in my strays."

"That's a damn lie. That old bitch is yanking your chain 'cause you and Sybil was close."

"Maybe so," Jake mused, "but you still got a thing for Sybil and everybody knows it."

"Listen," Gunther said, "I had Miss *high-n-mighty* Sybil Arkham when she was young, dumb and looking for

trouble. She's as dead to me now as her damned father."
Then he stood for a long, silent moment kicking at the
dirt. "But, it felt like she and I kinda deserved each other."

"Still might, if you're man enough," Jake taunted. "I
know a place and time she'll come running naked as a
jaybird through the woods with her dogs. I spied on her
a few times myself."

"Another damn lie!" Gunther shouted, slamming Jake
against the barn by the throat.

"You wanna bet?" Jake said. "You owes me big money
for helping kill Sybil's Hell hound, and I lost her friend-
ship to boot. So, for five hundred bucks, I'll tell where
and when."

"Alright, you lying sack of shit," Gunther said. "You're
on—where and when?"

"Well then," Jake said smiling, "tonight's gonna be the
full moon, ain't it?"

* * *

Dominique rolled the bones, Hester read her tea leaves
and Sybil dealt the Dark Tarot handed down in Arkham's
line from the old country. The signs were both auspicious
and dire—the same knife's edge Sybil had been walking
all her life. Only now she must act boldly and make haste.

Sybil held vigil night after night over Arturo's dog cage
in the basement among her wilder animals—until she witnessed his dreaming and finally knew what he was. He had
ample clothing now, so the garments and bedding he shredded were the proof she offered to her triad, gaining their

mixed blessings and predictions over what must unfold.

Sybil's fate now hinged on Arturo. Did he trust her? Would he obey? She had tested his nerve and hopefully whetted his appetite, but he was skittish and downtrodden from decades of abuse and exile south of the border. What lay ahead was dangerous and possibly fatal.

As the sun set in the west, and the full moon rose in the east, Sybil chased all her wild dogs out of the basement and into the woods. Her own guard dogs barked and howled from around the stone house to spur on their mad scramble. Then she unlocked Arturo's cage and dragged him out into the night.

"No, Señora Sybil, no!" he pleaded. "La noche es peligra, la Luna mas peligrosa!"

"Not tonight," Sybil said. "This night and this moon hold power." Then she used the voice Jake heard, her echoing voice of prophecy. ***"Go now Arturo, run free with the dogs."***

* * *

Jake was taking no chances. He'd plot and scheme, but always at others' expense. Tonight he and Gunther hid the van in a secluded, gravel clearing two hundred yards beyond the red barn. They were still on the edge of Sybil's wood, but Jake doubted her threat against him reached that far.

"She runs along the top of that wooded ridge," he told the Dutchman. "Hide somewhere up there until you hear her dogs pass by. That sweet-ass bitch will follow close behind, as naked as the day she was born, but a good deal more ripe for plucking."

"What about her dogs?" Gunther asked. "What if she sets them on me?"

"You got your handgun, right? Use it if you gotta, but try Sybil's magic, latin words first. They always worked for me."

"My people don't hold with magic," Gunther grumbled.

"Bullshit," Jake sneered. "Buggy jockeys are the most spooky fools I know. And you don't believe most of their holy-roller horseshit anyhow, as far as I can see."

"I don't follow much of it . . . but I still might believe," Gunther confessed.

"Well, believe this. If I was 'bout to rape somebody, I damn-sure wouldn't want no gunshot heard for miles around . . . unless you mean to kill her, like old man Arkham?"

"I never killed nobody! Don't ever say I did, or you'll be my first."

"Okay," Jake said. "I guess you just got rid of that old pickup out of youthful piety."

"I junked it when I joined the church—long after I dumped Sybil!" Gunther said. "You know real Amish ain't allowed to drive, that's why I pay you to haul my ass around."

"As I recall she dumped you—but you better get moving, or you'll lose her again."

The Dutchman started up the hill and soon vanished into the darkening woods. The sun disappeared and night came on. As the full moon loomed over the woodland, thousands of leaves shivered and rustled in the rising wind. All colors faded into black and shades of grey.

Jake sat huddled in the open side door of his van. All the van's lights were switched off. The only illumination came from the smoldering tip of Jake's cigarettes, which increased and diminished with each puff, exposing flashes of changing mood. Jake was a cautious soul, a patient observer of fate—particularly if it was not his own. Presently he heard Sybil's guard dogs bark and howl. The evening's entertainment had begun.

* * *

Gunther found a secure hideout behind a tangle of fallen trees. A flat area of woods spread out around him well illuminated by the moon. He could not be taken by surprise here. Shortly after he heard Sybil's dogs make a loud ruckus in the distance, a wave of assorted mutts came barreling through the landscape. There must have been over two dozen and they ran like they were being chased by the Devil himself.

Gunther hunched down and prayed they would not catch his scent. But they all raced on past as if they had been sent on a mission to somewhere else. Rising back up, the Dutchman prepared to ambush the proud beauty who bedeviled his dreams since tender youth. Tonight he would have Sybil again, make her his own forever, or end this torment for good.

Looking and listening intently for her approach, he heard instead a whimpering as if from a dog in pain and a strange, garbled stream of gibberish that sounded like prayer or confession. Coming out from behind the fallen trees into the open woods, he moved toward the sounds.

* * *

Jake had expected a little more action. Since the howling of Sybil's dogs he'd heard nothing. He began to consider possibilities in his mind, along with their consequences. *Maybe this was the wrong night.* The moon looked full, but what if it wasn't one hundred percent? Jake weren't no damn astrologer after all. *If it's the wrong night, Gunther will be pissed.*

Maybe Sybil didn't run every full Moon. Jake didn't know all the ins and outs of her kinky, mumbo-jumbo habits. What if it rained or snowed? What if she was on the rag? *Then Sybil won't show and Gunther will be pissed.* And these were only minor, possible pit-falls. Jake begin to weigh best and worst case scenarios against each other.

Maybe they would come together like lovers in a damn perfume commercial. Get all lovey-dovey and do it in the woods. Stroll back to her house and kick the Mex-can out. *If so, I'm stuck here all damn night, sleeping in the van, but eventually I'll get my money.*

Maybe Gunther will rape her. She'll fight back. Sybil ain't no patsy. He might even kill her. Jake hadn't heard a gun-shot, but one way or another Gunther would run back to the van to make his getaway . . . with Jake's help. *That will bring down a whole new world of trouble for me and the Dutchman.*

At that moment of sobering epiphany, Jake heard the

gunshot. He hopped to his feet, threw down his cigarette butt, then froze. All the butts he had smoked were evidence—with his own damn slobber all over them! He jumped back into the van, switched on the dome light so it would illuminate the area, then jumped back out and began franticly searching on his hands and knees in the gravel.

Finding all the butts, he thanked his lucky stars, just before noticing tiny reflections of the van's light in the dark woods. These were eyes, many, many pairs of animal eyes watching him crawl around like a damned fool. *Sybil's dog pack,* he thought. *I parked too close to the red barn!*

Jake jumped up and shouted "Cave Canem! Cave Canem!" as he was taught, which meant "Beware the Dog"—or perhaps *Beware the Alpha Bitch of Arkham,* Sybil herself. But these were not Sybil's guard dogs. These were the wild, stray dogs from her basement, dogs untrained and vicious. Dogs Jake captured and abused himself—and they were kept very hungry.

* * *

Up ahead Gunther made out the shadowy forms of two creatures struggling in the moonlight—a large, shaggy dog tightly held from behind by . . . something else. The dog whimpered and writhed as if in mortal pain. The thing that held it had bitten into the back of its neck with long, needle-like teeth—yet was whispering, or perhaps apologizing, in some unknown language to the poor animal as it died.

The Dutchman fired his gun into the air. The creature

released the dying dog and turned to face him. It had the frame of a smallish man, a gaunt, sunken build with a prominent row of spines erupting through the shredded shirt on its back. There was a vestigial tail and powerful hind legs thrusting out of the remains of ripped work jeans, and short, bony arms terminating in clawed hands. The face of the creature was nightmarish to behold: huge, yellow eyes, nose like a rat, long, pointed ears and a row of needle teeth that looked like they might overlap its quivering, bloated lower lip.

But the most horrible aspect—the feature making Gunther want to close his eyes even when in such obvious peril, was the creature's face, which seemed vaguely, irrationally human. "What the Hell are you?" Gunther shouted as he aimed his weapon at the creature.

"He is Arturo, my intended!" shouted a familiar voice somewhere behind him. Gunther turned his head, still holding his gun in the creature's direction. Sybil came straight at him, through the dark cathedral of towering trees, her voluptuous, naked body glistening in the moonlight, marked by weird black graffiti and the shifting, spiderweb shadows of overhead branches projected on her skin by the full moon.

"Have you never heard of a Chupacabra?" Sybil said, as she approached. "The Hispanic werewolf, the mysterious Goat Sucker that drains blood from farmers' flocks on nights like this."

"Never," Gunther said, lowering his gun and turning to face her. "For a second I was afraid it might be you,"

"No, not me, but not unlike me. You see Gunther,

unlike us—Arturo and I really have something in common." Gunther did not understand her, or the way she was changing before his eyes; her perfect body sprouting course, black fur, her feet and hands growing claws and her gorgeous face distorting, wolfish, inhuman—except for those piercing, azure eyes.

Too late, he understood why Sybil was different from other women. Too late, why the huge, black dog he ran over on Canal Road was her father. Too late, to save himself and use his gun on either creature. Needle teeth plunged into his neck from behind. Rapier claws slit his throat from ear to ear. He was slaughtered, torn into shreds like a ritual sacrifice at the feet of two apex, supernatural carnivores meeting-bloody for the first time under the light of a full moon.

"Tonight Arturo, my love," Sybil growled, **"you and I will create the next generation of Arkhams—or die trying."**

"What-the-hell is that?" Celine said.
"We call it the Erie Gate," I answered.
"It's the largest direct link between
Cleveland's sewers and the lake.
Impressive isn't it? Please note the
warning and no tresspassing signs—and
try to obey them."

Black Holes

"So what do you do?" said the young, Black woman casually smoking beside the entrance to City Hall. I'd been asked similar questions many times in the six months since I started working in Cleveland, but never by such an attractive interrogator.

"I'm with the Water Department," I said, noting she was not dressed or made up to impress, but managed to do so anyway.

"Really?" she replied, with muted disdain. "Don't be lying to me already."

"Okay, I'm with NEORSD, the Northeast Ohio Regional Sewer District."

"There you go Sparky," she teased, stubbing out her cigarette and flicking it into the nearby shrubbery. "I thought I caught a whiff of slide-rule geek about you." I was of course, a newly minted civil engineer. Our electronic calculators do all the math now days, but I kept my father's ivory & walnut slide rule in my desk for luck. I never expected anyone to smell that.

"And what is it that you do, Miss . . . ?"

"I investigate things. You may call me Celine."

"Well, I'm Bill Carson and I inspect things. So we're in the same business."

"Hardly," she huffed. "You got a ticket for this dog and pony show?"

"Absolutely," I said, showing my conference pass. "I did the Power Point visuals."

"Good for you, Sparky. I'm about to become your plus one."

The conference room was filling up as we entered. The young Mayor, Justin Bibb and the new County Commissioner, Chris Ronayne were jockeying for dominance up on the podium among a slew of other officials, including my superiors at NEORSD. Still, our own lowly entrance and seating far back in the auditorium drew considerable attention. I thought it was because of the beautiful woman at my side, never imagining the actual cause of her prominence.

"This is a great day for our city," the Mayor proclaimed. "Today we begin the final phase of Cleveland's Wastewater Control Project to achieve one hundred percent compliance with the EPA's Clean Water Act—our streams, our river, our lake and our city will never be cleaner and healthier!" A fair degree of ritual applause followed before a string of government suits began taking credit for infrastructure improvements, federal grants, zoning changes and contract negotiations. In truth, none of them had so much as lifted a shovel. A previous Governor, Mayor and Commissioner had cracked the whips that got this ball rolling.

It was all pretty much white noise for me and I could tell Celine was also progressively less enthralled. What did excite me, once the lights were lowered, was the visual presentation; the maps, graphs, rainfall projections and statistics I had slaved over. I was particularly proud of the color scheme—beige background, black streets, blue waterways and the green sewer grid with the underground catch basins and twenty-two miles of new tunnel that made it all work.

"Nice artwork Sparky," Celine whispered provocatively into my ear. "The green sewers are pure genius . . . baby-shit brown would have totally spoiled the mood."

When the lights came back up, project officials asked for questions and the local media lobbed them verbal softballs they could clobber out of the park with pre-rehearsed talking points. Finally the Mayor asked, "Will that be all?" and Celine stood up. A hushed, low moan escaped from the podium and assembled media.

"I'd like to ask something," Celine said, in loaded, sugary tones.

"Of course you would," the County Commissioner muttered sarcastically. "We all feared you might skip this Saturday conference Celine, in observance of Shabbat with your father."

"But instead," Celine purred. "Old Saul sent me here to observe all of you."

"Go ahead and speak, Miss Goldberg," the Mayor sighed.

"I wish to know why our city is spending *BILLIONS* of taxpayer dollars to dig gigantic *CESS POOLS* and useless *WORM HOLES* beneath our neighborhoods?" she shouted, causing a wave of shocked gulps and nervous giggles to wash over the assembled crowd.

"They are *NOT* cess pools, they are *CATCH BASINS*

for excess, tainted rain water," the Commissioner barked back. "And these are all *FEDERAL* funds from the Infrastructure Act!"

"Federal funds are still taxpayer dollars Commissioner, unless you think Washington just prints money in the White House basement." Celine said, in a most rational slander. "And that *RAIN WATER* will be tainted with *RAW SEWAGE*, which smells as nasty as any *CESS POOL!*"

After that there was nothing for me to do but quickly shepherd her toward the door while the rest of the conference disintegrated into chaotic, armed camps. On the front steps we both took a breather looking back toward the raucous melee inside.

"Well," I said, "that's one way to spark rigorous debate."

"Think I cost you a job?" she asked.

"No, I barely exist back at headquarters, but security heads might roll."

"You ever been down in those tubes?"

"You mean in the actual city sewers?"

"Yes Sparky, is this London? Do we have a real subway? Of course I mean the sewers."

"Well no, I inspect pressure valves and monitor bacteria counts at the treatment plants."

"Then it's high time you got your hands dirty. Are you normally in observance on a Sunday morning Mr. Billy White-bread?"

"Well, I'm country-club Methodist, so . . . not unless it's Christmas or Easter."

"Good," she said. "Then meet me Sunday morning at

Civilization Coffee House in Tremont. We'll take a little tour. Lose the suit, dress for hiking and wear waterproof boots."

With that, she pranced down the front steps, retrieved her dirt bike from the ornamental shrubbery where she stashed it, kicked it into life and sped away down Lakeside Avenue. I just stood there watching her disappear until Mr. Vortees placed a meaty hand on my shoulder.

"Nice catch," he said, in his slobbery accent I could never quite identify. "You're a fast worker."

"I didn't work at all," I admitted. "She hooked me at the door."

"Used you to get inside did she? Clever girl, that one—a clever, dangerous girl." At this point I felt reluctantly compelled to turn and face my direct supervisor. Facing Mr. Athol Vortees was never easy as he suffered major burns in childhood, presenting a hairless, melted face, blood-shot eyes and grotesque, lipless smile. He also gave off pungent odors from eyewash and ointments he frequently required. I had to suppress an instinctive flinch at our every encounter.

"Is she really a Goldberg?" I asked.

"Adopted obviously, along with her brother," he sneered.

"Should I avoid them from now on?"

"Avoid her brother, he's an ACLU lawyer and Black-Lives-Matter thug. Their old, toothless father, Saul is a world-class, liberal troublemaker," he said. "But stick to Celine like her tramp stamp. No doubt she believes you're infatuated and will attempt to pump you for information.

Are you infatuated, Mr. Carson?"

"No sir, she's not exactly my type."

"Good, then pump her instead. Enjoy it if you can, but learn what she knows, where she goes and who she tells about it. Then report back to me."

* * *

"You call those hiking boots?" said the tall, leggy beauty draped over a chair outside the coffee house. She was wearing what looked like army surplus, but maybe Israeli army surplus because everything was cut off, rolled up or unbuttoned for maximum, hot-weather comfort.

"They're all I own," I admitted. "I'm not going to buy new boots just to wade in a sewer. I'm not much of an outdoorsy guy."

"Are they even waterproof?"

"No, I put plastic bags over my socks and have a pair of loafers back in my car."

"Jeez Sparky, you got some full-grown-man stuff going on, like your nice build and your engineering job, but you act like you still live in your parent's basement."

"I own a condo in Ohio City and I work out—at a gym—inside."

"Not my American Dream, but okay. Let's get going."

"I thought we were getting together for breakfast before our hike."

"You thought wrong. This isn't eHarmony White-bread, we're on a mission. Now grab a coffee and a frigging tea-cake and let's go."

* * *

The coffee was strong, the tea-cake proved stale and our forced march down the Towpath Trail North into Canal Basin Park was anything but leisurely. I did enjoy the utilitarian grandeur of the new highway bridges overhead, but Celine pointed out the huge amount of rubble from older demolished neighborhoods now used as ornamental landscaping beneath those structures.

"Winners and losers, Sparky," she said. "All the folks that lived here are gone now."

As the trail bottomed out along the river, we took a weedy right turn to arrive at an overgrown, chain-link fence topped with barbed-wire. Two weathered plaques proclaimed this to be Walworth Run, a notorious industrial creek and open sewer. The evils of overflow drainage pollution and the 1969 Cuyahoga River Fire were also calamitously evoked.

"Shame we can't get down there," I said, anticipating an honorable retreat.

"Don't you wish," she said. "Come on, follow me."

"But it's fenced off. There are No Trespassing signs—in English and Spanish."

"On whose orders?" she said, clearly pointing to the answer on these signs.

"The Northeast Ohio Regional Sewer District." I read aloud.

"Which YOU frigging work for, right? So we're good to go!" Celine then sprinted down the fence line to where it protruded four feet out over the river. She grabbed the end fence post with both hands using her momentum to swing around over the water and land gracefully atop a concrete retaining wall on the other side. I managed the same with much more effort.

We walked back inland atop the retaining wall and climbed down to the mostly dry stream bed. Before us loomed the yawning, stone-encased mouth of Walworth Run. Celine opened the smallish military shoulder bag she carried and produced a pair of elastic strap headlamps, two NK95 masks, ubiquitous since the recent pandemic, and a Beretta 9mm pistol.

"You brought a weapon?" I gasped.

"It's cool," she said. "I got a carry permit and know how to use it from the army. Old Saul raised my brother and me in Israel where every kid—boys and girls, join the military. Gal Gadot and I are like kick-ass sisters." She laughed at her Hollywood reference while stashing the Beretta under the belt of her shorts at the ass-crack and concealing it with her loose, unbuttoned army shirt. "Besides, you gotta carry something to fight off the CHUD."

"The what?" I said.

"Cannibalistic Humanoid Underground Dwellers."

"Oh *HELL* no!" I shouted, turning to climb back up the retaining wall.

"I'm joking! That's from an old horror movie about New York City. Some homeless do live in these tunnels, but only in cold weather. Jeez Sparky, where the heck did you grow up?"

"Farmland . . . Indiana, it's about twenty miles east of Muncie."

"So . . . *Children Of The Corn* would be more your fright-night movie speed?"

She wasn't wrong, but our entrance into this entombed stream reminded me more of *Journey To The Center Of The Earth.* There was no disagreeable stench here as it was flushed regularly with street runoff. The toxic, mixed sewer configuration would appear deeper in.

I tried explaining the system to Celine by comparing it to human circulation. The largest tunnels are like major arteries near the heart, with smaller and smaller passages branching out to the body of our city. The smallest capillaries would be the various lines to our sinks and toilets.

"Are you talking blood or shit in this urban cadaver?" she asked.

"Both really. Fresh water from Lake Erie is the lifeblood of Cleveland. It's sucked from the Five-mile Crib, which is that far out to avoid filth flowing from the Cuyahoga into the lake. Then it's pumped uphill to Baldwin Reservoir near Shaker Heights, where it's purified. From there it flows downhill to everybody's faucets where it's used before going down some drain."

"Then it becomes shit?" she said.

"*Waste water* technically, but yes. You drink it after that—you get sick or die."

Then I talked her through the dark side of the equation. Shit and piss, like water, flow downhill through ever larger pipes and passages toward our river and lake. But just before we piss where we drink (and only in the last one hundred fifty years), we capture it at filtration plants and purify it, before dumping it into the Cuyahoga River and Lake Erie again.

"Could we drink it then?"

"I wouldn't, and this is why." We had just come upon the first of many side tunnels branching off of Walworth Run. Before us lay the notorious design flaw in nineteenth century sanitary technology—the mixed use sewer. Constructed of red brick and concrete it presented a cross section of one large open-topped channel, in which we now stood, for rainwater from the streets, lawns and rooftops above—and a much smaller, open-topped channel running along half- way up the wall for toxic, raw sewage which required us to hurriedly employ our masks.

"Ew, why'd they run them together?" Celine choked.

"Lower cost, greater access," I admitted. "Why dig two trenches when you can dig one? And why enclose the channels when they are easier to clean and maintain if open?"

"Because it stinks like Hell down here—that's why!"

"I assure you, the design engineers were *NOT* the folks working down here."

"I've seen and smelled enough," she said, interrupting my tutorial. I held her back for one more moment to visually demonstrate the entire purpose of the Wastewater Control Project which first brought us together.

"If it rains enough to reach this level," I demonstrated with my hand just above the top of the smaller channel. "Then street water mixes with sewage and it all flushes into the lake. That's why we're building the retention basins—to catch that overflow."

"One must be close then," she said, just noticing footprints in the mud at our feet.

Indeed, many tracks covered the muddy floor leading both to and from the river. Only a few could be ours. The others seemed to turn and enter the many branching tunnels to our left.

"We should follow them!" she said. "I'll scratch a mark on the tunnel walls with my gun so we don't get lost." I had a sick feeling in my gut, but Celine was hot on the trail. I followed reluctantly hoping she had spare batteries for our headlamps and didn't notice the tracks we followed were not familiar boot marks, but unshod feet with oddly webbed toes.

* * *

The footprints led relentlessly upward, at first branching to the left, then right and left again. At each juncture I made sure Celine scratched a mark, unsure if she or I could remember and retrace our steps to the river.

Eventually we must have climbed high enough to get out of the Cuyahoga Valley and under city streets. The holes in street drains and manholes above us provided scattered light. I had no idea what neighborhood we were under, but our upward slant somewhat diminished right up until stopping abruptly.

Before us was an iron gate, encrusted with wet, hanging streamers of trash and vegetation. It looked like a circular prison door with horizontal and vertical bars cross-welded to restrict everything but the eight-inch sewage channel— and we certainly weren't going to crawl through that.

"I think it opens," Celine said. "These are hinges and over here must be a lock." We both scraped at the muck and trash fouling the mechanism and found a keyhole. "It's either locked or rusted shut," she said after vigorous shaking. "Do they give you some kind of company key?"

"No! I can't even imagine why there ARE locked partitions down here. It goes against the whole idea of clear drainage." We shined our headlamps through the grating, illuminating fifty feet of tunnel ending in a larger chamber containing a curved metal wall. "Maybe this is one of the finished retention basins," I guessed. "Only a quarter of the total are still to be built."

"What does a basin look like?" Celine wondered. "Is it like a big bowl or something?"

"No, it's designed like a cylinder a few hundred feet in diameter and buried in the ground. Imagine a gigantic coffee can six to eight hundred feet deep. It would connect to massive filling and draining tunnels and have powerful pumps to force water in or out."

"Let's try shooting this lock open!" Celine said with alarming glee.

"Don't do that!" I shouted. "We're not here to destroy company property. What if the bullet ricochets in this tunnel and hits one of us?"

"You big pussy. Who said you get to decide?" Nobody obviously, and with a wildcat like Celine, I don't know why I thought I could. Still, I couldn't allow her to breach NEORSD security, so I grabbed both her arms to keep her from using her Beretta.

"You like playing rough, Sparky?" she said, just before

kneeing me in the groin. I doubled up in pain, but still held her arms. Using my body weight I pinned her against the tunnel wall to keep her from hurting me again.

As we wrestled, a metallic, grinding sound came from somewhere behind the gate. We both looked toward it as a gush of water bubbled up from around the metal wall and raced toward us. It was already six inches deep by the time it reached our feet.

"Let's go!" I yelled. "We can fight later." As I pulled away she grabbed my arm.

"Billy, don't leave me—I don't know how to swim." Her's was a startling mood reversal I didn't have time to savor, as now knee-deep current chased us down the tunnel slope.

We both lost our footing and floundered onward, sometimes rolling like beach balls in the now waist-deep flood. As I struggled to keep our heads above water I realized we would soon be swept below street level and plunge into darkness and ever stronger downhill current. Certainly we'd both drown before reaching the river.

Grabbing one of the iron ladder rungs imbedded in the tunnel wall, which led up to every manhole, I caught Celine by the waist as she flushed by. "Grab these loops and climb." I yelled over the rushing flood. "I'll get us out of here somehow."

Climbing above the immediate peril, I realized I would not be able to force the manhole cover with both of us on this meager ladder. Luckily, a street drain was only a few feet from the manhole. I told Celine to hang onto the drain slits and keep her face up to the grating for air.

Letting the water lift my whole body to nearly the top of the ladder I positioned my back and shoulders against the manhole cover. I applied maximum pressure with both legs on the next to the top rung and strained with all my might. Miraculously, I popped the steel cover loose.

Of course if a car had come along at that moment I might have been sliced in half emerging above the pavement. Thank God the street was empty. I was able to shove the lid away, jump back in holding firmly to the rim with one hand and fish Celine to safety as the tunnel filled completely and began to overflow out of the open manhole and drain grating.

We sat like drowned rats on the blacktop, water flowing all around us. Looking up I realized we were on a street off Scranton Road, four blocks from where I parked my car. "Come on," I said. "I'll drive you to my condo where we can shower and get dry clothes."

"Oh no," she said. "I'm not that damn grateful. It's time you talked with the boys."

* * *

Her family home was one of those used-to-be prosperous, grand houses in Cleveland Heights. I parked my costly Tesla on the street and hoped it would survive. The front seats were already trashed from our wet and muddy clothes, but my new Tesla had failed to impress Celine anyway.

We were met at the door by a tall, handsome, Black man who looked like he could have gone one-on-one with

Mike Tyson. Celine blew past him, tossing off minimal introductions in her wake.

"This is my older brother Marcus. Marcus, this is Sparky, the guy from the sewer department who nearly got us both killed—but then saved my life."

"Whoa," I stammered. "That was not at all . . ."

"Relax, Dude," he said. "I know my sister exaggerates. What's your real name?"

"Bill Carson, I work for NEORSD and I barely know your sister."

"She's quite a trip, isn't she?" he said. "But be warned Billy, you mess with her and she *WILL* kick your ass. Now let me show you the utility bathroom in the basement. Celine will take up the one upstairs for hours. You can shower and I'll bring you some of my clothes. After that you both will have to deal with Old Saul."

Why Old Saul, their adoptive father was such a threat I didn't know. He looked like an ancient Al Pacino with coke-bottle-thick glasses. However, he reigned like a Biblical prophet from an overstuffed chair by the fireplace in their living room, with Celine and I seated before him on the carpet and Marcus standing off to one side like court security.

"So children," Saul said, "are you two together now?"

"No," we both said with differing degrees of certainty.

"It's alright young man. I know my *meshuggah* daughter sleeps around."

"Dad," Celine shouted. "I'm just using him to get info on this Retention Basin bullshit!"

"Harsh my daughter, but also honest. And how do you

feel about that, Mr. Carson?"

"Umm . . . I'm not totally surprised?"

"Good, you kids can kiss and make up later. Now," Saul said, "tell me about the basins."

I ran down most of what I knew about the Wastewater Control Project, the EPA regulations and Cleveland's historic shortcomings at controlling pollution in the river and lake. Saul had numerous questions including the construction, operation and locations of the system.

"I'm afraid I'm not familiar with all the particulars," I admitted.

"Bullshit, he's lying!" Celine said. "He drew up an entire map they showed at City Hall."

"Again, I apologize for my daughter's mouth," Saul said. "But is this true, Mr. Carson?"

"Yes and no," I said. "I drew the map. But it was just a drawing, not really accurate or to scale. I was supposed to make the system look good—for the public. I'm not a real expert."

"I understand," Saul said. "But will the basins really solve these pollution problems?"

I took a minute to reflect. I work for NEORSD, but they don't exactly pay me to outright lie.

"No," I said. "It will get the EPA off Cleveland's back for the foreseeable future, but with agricultural runoff, garbage from other lakes flowing downstream, forever chemicals and micro plastics, Lake Erie is basically doomed in the long run." On that note Saul's court took a turn.

"Mr. Carson was honest with us," Saul said. "Now children, let's be straight with him."

"We think the basins are a lie," Marcus started. "A plot to steal excess water for sale."

"The Great Lakes hold like a fifth of all the fresh water in the world," Celine added. "The Midwest states like Ohio control it, but Texas and the southwestern states need and want it—and probably have the political pull to siphon it away from us."

"However," Saul advised, "Canada also owns half the water in these lakes and has a mutual treaty with the United States not to take any more water from the lakes than local cities and industries need. So Mr. Carson, let us ask, what is a capitalist city like Cleveland to do?"

"Umm . . . make a new treaty?" I guessed.

"Or share the money with Canada," Marcus reasoned.

"Or go to fucking war on another border!" Celine declared.

"Or maybe we dig these huge reservoirs (for pollution control let us say)," Saul proposed. "Then we fill them up with lake water over and over, which somehow magically disappears (on a regular basis), to Texas."

"Well," I murmured hesitantly, "I guess that could be theoretically possible?"

"Good, good," Saul said. " We agree to disagree—now we can eat."

* * *

I spent the night in Cleveland Heights alone on a couch. When I got up Celine was gone, "back with her girlfriend in Tremont." My clothes were washed and dried, and everything in my wallet was laid on a towel to dry out next to Celine's disassembled Beretta. Her cell phone was in a bag of rice, but they didn't find mine. Flushed down to the river, I guess.

I spent some time cleaning the seats in my Tesla. Marcus commented on how much I must earn at NEORSD, but I explained they subsidize our transportation to "go green" as much as possible. Later, back in my condo, I discovered unpleasant odors and unexpected company.

"How did you get in here?"

"We were worried when you didn't show up for work," Mr. Vortees said. "The police got management to open your door."

"Afraid you actually killed both of us?"

"My dear Mr. Carson, you tripped an alarm. The security response is automatic. I had nothing to do with it. But since you survived, what have you learned from the Goldbergs?"

"They know nothing—think we're hoarding lake water in the basins to sell to Texas or elsewhere to work around our Canadian treaty," I said. "They're left-wing conspiracy crazies."

"How interesting. We should consider that as a back-up agenda. It's much easier to interest the public in corruption than conservation."

"Do yourself a favor, take a television crew out touring the new locations," I said. "Show the public our big empty holes. They'll lose interest quickly."

"I'll consider it. Meanwhile, we found your phone," he said, tossing it at me. "It got wet."

* * *

I passed the next month dealing with fires I had started. No television crew wanted to cover our new sewer construction. Even neighborhood kids would not stand around watching us dig holes to China. Conversely, cities all over the Great Lakes wanted clandestine briefings about our imaginary Texas water conspiracy. They all craved a piece of the action—even in Canada.

Back home at last, I was working out in my gym at street level on Detroit Avenue when nobody's favorite rabble-rouser came rapping on the floor to ceiling windows.

"Hey Sparky, you're looking suitably buff and sweaty."

"What do you want Celine? I'm kind of busy right now."

"I want Honey Hut ice cream down at Edgewater Beach."

"Not a nice, long, mile swim?" I suggested.

"You know better. Come on, you've already nearly wearing swim trunks." It turns out she wasn't interested in ice cream or water sports. She wanted more information. "What-the-hell is this?" she said, standing before a huge, ominous, circular, Edgewater Beach anomaly.

"We call it The Erie Gate," I said. "It's the largest direct link between the sewers and the lake. Impressive isn't it? Please note the warning and no trespass signs—and try to obey them."

"Looks like a Bond villain hideout. How heavy is that steel door and how does it open?"

"Two tons I'd guess. Water pressure opens it—but it

would take a real monsoon to do it."

"Ever seen it open?" she wondered.

"Nobody has, because nobody *SANE* visits the beach during a torrential downpour!"

* * *

Celine and I fell into something almost like dating. We had each other's phone numbers. She reappeared between stays with her girlfriend. I wasn't courting her, but Vortees ordered me to stay in touch. Truthfully, I'd much rather touch her brother. That was my dark secret—why I left Indiana, why I shun church and why I moved to Cleveland where such longings are *theoretically possible.*

So when Celine said she was ready for a sleepover, I was really in turmoil. Even worse, she wanted us to go on a camp out.

"I told you I'm not outdoorsy."

"I got all the stuff we need, and you can share my sleeping bag," she teased. "Our co-ed boot camps used to get really, really frisky out in the Negev Desert."

"All right," I said, planning to dodge it on some other pretext. "How far out of town? I'm not familiar with Ohio parks."

"Edgewater Park this weekend."

"Nobody is even allowed *IN* the park after dark," I complained. "And it's supposed to rain cats and dogs all the way from Friday night through Monday morning."

"I know," she said. "It will be awesome!"

This was obviously not about passion, but her desire

to see the Erie Gate open. I tried begging off, but she was adamant. And yes, I'd been with women before, in high school, before I stopped lying to myself. So, as a last resort, I'd flag a park ranger and get us both arrested.

After work Friday, I parked the Tesla up in Battery Park where it was upscale enough to blend in. We carried our stuff in through the W.76th street tunnel and set up her camouflaged tent in a dense thicket on the wooded hillside above the Erie Gate just before dark.

As the park rangers chased everyone out after sunset, we walked over to Don's Lighthouse Grille on Clifton to eat dinner and nurse drinks until ten thirty. I'd never seen Celine drink before, but she tossed them down like a sailor. At eleven we snuck back into the park, keeping to the woods until we were comfortably under her tent. About midnight it started to rain.

It wasn't cool enough for her sleeping bag, so we unzipped it and used it as a cover. About the time we removed most of our clothing Celine made the first move.

"Billy," she said, which was a noticeable recent upgrade from calling me Sparky, "I know I've made you wait awhile, and you've been really patient."

"Which happens when I get kneed in the nuts from the get-go."

"Sorry, that was my military training. They taught girls that and other things to deal with bad men. I know you're not like that Billy, but tonight I need you to be a little more aggressive."

I was apprehensive. I would've confessed, but I keep so much hidden besides that, it was safer to just pretend.

Luckily, I'd read up on oral foreplay, which seemed to satisfy her anyway.

* * *

When I woke it'd been pouring for hours and Celine was gone. Getting dressed I noticed she left her shoulder bag. It was empty except for extra ammunition. I crawled out to search, finding her behind a tree near the Erie Gate.

"It's all the way open," she whispered.

"Has it rained that much?" I said.

"No. A ton of water's flowing out, but something else is going on."

The park and beach were dark under dense rain clouds rolling in from the North. But the lights from the freeway and downtown back lit an astounding, shadowy procession marching out of the lake. Several dozen dark figures struggled and strained to drag and push an immense, bulbous something toward the open gate.

"Who are they and what-the-hell is that?" Celine said, her muted voice almost hysterical.

"I have no idea," I lied.

This company of darkness struggled across the sand, using the water flowing from the gate as lubrication under their burden. Celine and I watched as they disappeared into the tunnel beyond the gate. Some wavering illumination leaked forth from inside as they lit their way further inside. Their shadows, spilling back over the beach, cast a grotesque dance of squirming, amorphous monstrosity.

"Let's go!" Celine said, exiting the cover of the tree to

follow them.

"We are *NOT* going in there!" I said as forcefully as possible while still whispering.

"You may not Sparky, but I will." she said, scrambling onto the beach. Of course I followed. It's what men do—reluctant, stupid, doomed men. Once in the tunnel I could see the struggling, monstrous group far ahead and Celine's Beretta stuffed in her waistband as before.

We tried being stealthy, but the foot-deep water flowing out of the tunnel, and the tendency of enclosed places to produce echos, betrayed us. The group in front stopped. A slobbering, not totally unfamiliar voice shouted, "Waagla, vaas wahsaag?" Silence followed. Celine and I froze in place for several tense moments, barely daring to breathe. "Woldaa, Vaarg!" shouted the voice and the group plodded forward. *I caught a faint, vile odor among the general stench and I knew. I knew but I dared not say. How could I ever explain that to Celine?* We tried to match them stride for stride, but took one errant, sloshy step too far.

"Who's there?" the voice slobbered again, and a dozen blue-green lights turned in our direction blinding us. "It's you two idiots!" the voice declared. "Why can't you ever learn to leave well enough alone?"

We switched on our own headlamps and there before us was the most preposterous horror imaginable: a nightmare tableau of dozens of amphibious humanoids dressed in clothing of woven seaweed and fish scales, attending a gigantic, unknown species of freshwater cephalopod which glared back at us in anger with enormous yellow eyes and writhing, suckered tentacles. And there, commanding them all was Athol Vortees—whose stench and voice I'd recognized.

I thought I had never seen creatures like these before, but I was wrong. I had known one from my very first day on the job. The disfigured visage of Athol Vortees was not the result of childhood tragedy. It was an ingeniously flawed attempt to make him appear human. A result so skillfully inept, so horribly botched, it succeeded in avoiding all polite inquiry.

"Seen enough Miss Goldberg?" Athol said. "It's the last thing you'll ever see. How sad you could not appreciate our achievement, the glorious subjugation of a city, of an entire region to preserve our ancient ones, the memory and soul of our Vaarg race. You've built them a new underground sanctuary from our threatened home—the Great Lake you poison with your filth!"

As Vortees and his minions advanced upon us, Celine reached back for her weapon. But I had already snatched it and backed off a few steps toward the beach.

"What are you doing?" she screamed. "Give me that!"

"I can't," I said.

"Then shoot them, they're monsters. Kill them all!"

"I can't," I said. "I work for them. They are NEORSD."

The look in her eyes as she found me out was brutal. Almost as brutal as her leaping, roundhouse kick which should have broken my neck. But Celine was a little drunk, was standing in a foot of water, and I felt it coming. I flinched back, her kick missed and the Beretta fired.

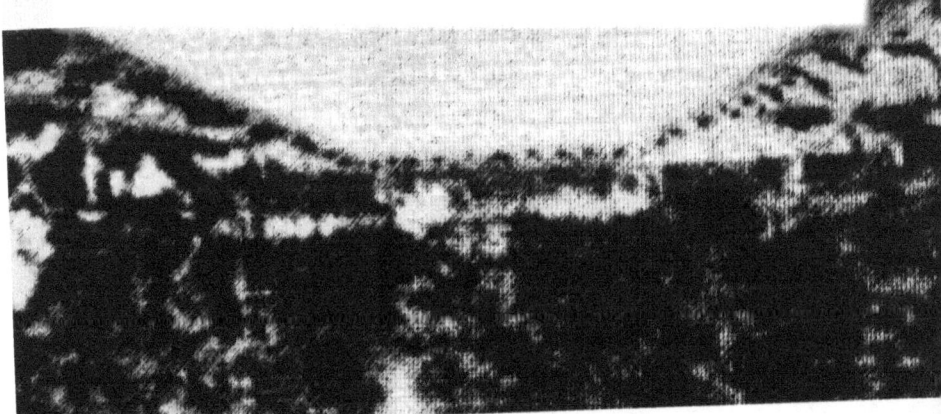

Strategically buried behind the ticket counter, snack bar and souvenir emporium was a "History of The Blue Hole" display with its improbable timeline, antique photographs and artistic rendering of the "Native American" burials discovered below.

Fair Exchange

The warm sun at my back, the bluest of waters ahead and the calm surroundings could not elevate my frame of mind. This placid, almost celebratory location for most was a virtual cemetery for me and a mausoleum for those below. Our company had done an amazing job redeveloping this place given the circumstances; artificially limited time, vastly over budget and under mortal distress. But I found no solace in any of that.

My accustomed perch atop one of those "plasticized" picnic tables faced the boardwalk circling the pond, with its lush flower beds and sturdy pier stretching out to a floating observation deck railed off for tourists wanting to gaze deep into the mysteries below. It also faced a commemorative plaque with the names of the dead and a brief summation of their demise. This is what happens when personal tragedy becomes history and history is marketed as myth.

The myth was casually enshrined in the new Blue Hole Visitor Center located at the far edge of the parking lot behind me. Strategically buried behind the ticket counter, snack bar and souvenir emporium was a "History of The Blue Hole" display with its improbable time line, antique newspaper articles, photographs and a small section of the mysterious copper net—along with artistic "renderings"of the "Native American" burials discovered below. Somewhere hidden in all that white-washed boilerplate was a blurry picture of Frank and I seated in a small submarine.

"I warned you to stay away," growled the ominous, husky shadow blocking out all warmth behind me. "Don't make me call the cops again."

"I bought a ticket." I said, without looking back at my aged transgressor. "Perhaps I should have you arrested for discrimination against the civil and educated."

"Over-educated you mean. I'd refund double just to kick your smart ass out. You're persona-non-grata around here Stern." As I turned to face this corporate enforcer I recalled the persona he assumed at our first meeting, a portly Grandpa McCoy with a warm smile and country twang. Now Mr. Webb seemed more mafia boss with dark suit, ham fists and menacing sneer—apparently a chameleon for all reasons.

"Just paying my respects," I said, indicating the plaque. I'll be going now."

"Not so fast," Webb said, blocking me with a meaty palm to the chest. "Somebody else wants a word." He stepped aside revealing a smallish young woman poised behind him. To say she was striking seems inadequate. Her spiky, multi-hued, "mermaid" hair was cause enough, but the rich, olive skin tone, large green eyes, full wide lips and shapely yoga outfit really sealed the deal.

"Hello Dr. Stern," she cooed, in a voice more low and resonate than her stature suggested. "I've been wanting to make your acquaintance." Brushing aside her gruff chaperone, She extended one slender hand with curiously long fingers and almost nonexistent nails. Shaking hello, I found her touch unusually cool despite the temperature of the day.

"Should I know you Miss," I said. "Are you enrolled in one of my classes?"

"Ha! Give it up Romeo," Webb croaked in disdain. "She's not nearly as green as she looks!" The little lady shot a sideways glance and a dismissive gesture toward her companion. He quickly retreated behind her.

"Sorry," I said. "It seems your boss and I have some bad blood between us."

"She's my boss, Stern," Mr.Webb said, nudging his suit jacket open just enough to display a peek of shoulder holster and gun handle. "Show her proper respect."

"That will be enough," she said without looking back. "You may go." Her chided underling relaxed his stance, turned and walked back to the Visitors Center. "Let's take a seat Professor," she said smiling. "Unlike my subordinate, I prefer to play nice."

I sat down on the side of the picnic table with my back toward the pond. She chose the same side, hopped up on the seat and squatted cross-legged on the table top—seizing the high ground as it were. This gave me a rather intimate view of her attire including the bulky plastic Crocs that made her feet look wildly disproportionate.

"Mind if I smoke?" she said, pulling a pack of menthols and lighter from a stylish shoulder purse seemingly constructed of metallic fish scales.

"Not at all," I said. "Although I hear it may stunt your

growth."

"Good one!" she chortled. "But you're not exactly a basketball player yourself. Look, I know it's a filthy habit—that's why I like it. I always dreamed of breathing fire." Then she took a long drag, threw her head back and blew out a cloud of hot vapor. "My name is Marina Vaarg. I think we had a mutual . . . friend?"

I couldn't imagine who that might be. Certainly if anyone I knew met such an exotic creature as she, they would have informed me with breathless enthusiasm.

"I surrender to your superior social connections."

"Does the name Richard Ivers ring any bells?" she said. But of course it did - alarm bells, visions of inky blackness and a mind-altering fear of death.

"The manager of the salt mine . . . under Lake Erie," I shuttered, looking up at her with a growing sense of dread.

"Former manager," She said, studying my reaction closely. "Sadly he passed away recently—industrial accident. Lakeline Corporation controls the salt mine now."

It suddenly became clear who controlled Lakeline Corp. and what they were doing at The Blue Hole. Perhaps their tentacles spread all over Lake Erie's watershed from Toledo to Buffalo. I saw no reason to imagine it stopped there... *Canada, Michigan, New York, perhaps the entire Great Lakes?*

I rose abruptly, tripped while extricating myself from the picnic table and staggered over to steady myself against the bronze plaque, (Frank and Jim's memorial), another permanent reminder of my unforgivable incompetence.

"I guess you didn't know," she said, watching my distress, gauging how far she could push me. "Richard told me all about you, about your little adventure together, about poor Henry Danforth and about what you found."

"I . . . don't umm . . . know what you're talking about," I stammered.

"We think you do, Professor. Imagine our surprise finding you involved out here, making another discovery—with more unfortunate friends. Your social circle seems a bit terminal, wouldn't you say?"

"What do you want from me?" I gasped, stepping back on the boardwalk .

"I want what you took from the salt mine," She said, crushing out her cigarette on the table top. "The creature belongs with us."

"Well you can't have it!" I shouted. "I gave it all to NASA. All of it, the frozen specimen, the photographs, the drawings and all my feeble attempts at a translation. It's all top secret now. Why else do you think they hired someone like me?"

"We wondered about that also." she said, before I ran to my car and sped away.

* * *

After my confrontation at The Blue Hole, I barricaded myself in my apartment for a week, cancelled all my classes and called in sick at NASA. I even considered moving out of state and buying a firearm. Then, late Saturday night, someone rang my buzzer.

The front door camera showed some teenager in a dark hoodie. I never ordered Door-Dash so I used the intercom. "Who is it?" I said.

"It's Marina—what's up Doc?" an all-too-familiar voice answered, and I went into a tailspin of anguished regret. *Why didn't I move to Colorado? They have loads of cheap handguns!*

"Why are you here?"

"Remedial Dating 101," she said. "You forgot to ask for my number."

Shit, shit, double shit! I don't even want . . .Jesus! I freaked and refused to buzz her in. I decided to totally ignore her, sit on the floor with my back against the door, maybe buy a bus ticket tomorrow. Five minutes later she was rapping on the door.

"Who let you inside the lobby?" I shouted through the door.

"Kevin and Nora from down the hall, a fun young couple. I said you were advising on my dissertation; *Intergenerational Sex Techniques In The Late Anthropocene.* They were happy to let me in—said you don't get out nearly enough."

"How did you find me?" I asked, not that it mattered because she was here.

"You think Richard Ivers didn't know where you lived?" she said. "Professor, you gave him everything, even your blood type and Social Security number."

"But nobody was ever supposed to reveal that!"

"You're the fool who signed all his corporate, non-disclosure bullshit—he didn't sign anything," she said. "Now get off the floor and let's take care of business."

"What business." I said, opening the door. "I told you I gave everything to NASA, or is it time for you to murder the last eye witness?"

"Do I look like an assassin?" she said, displaying her exuberant attire. The inside of her shiny black hoodie was lined in fuzzy fuchsia, she wore a thin spaghetti-strap top and Beatles' Yellow Submarine sweat pants. As before her shoes were the coup-de-gras, large hairy house slippers that resembled bear claws.

"You could use . . . I don't know . . . your poisonous blue lipstick or something."

"Ooow," she teased, "Now he wants to kiss me! Why do you think I want to kill you Sam? Or should I always use Dr. *Samuel* Stern, which sounds kinda stand-offish."

"Because you've murdered everyone else!" I shouted.

"But did we?"

"You murdered Henry Danforth!"

"Well yes, we did, but he shoved a ten foot rebar through the body of a sleeping prehistoric criminal (the very existence of which is now top secret), so I'd consider that as obvious self-defense."

"You killed Jim Stevenson."

"Jim who?"

"The crane operator."

"Your operator died from careless use of construction equipment—ask OSHA."

"Richard Ivers?"

"Ivers was run down by a front end loader carrying rock salt. It was in the newspaper. You've been in that salt mine, it'a a death trap down there."

"And none of that had anything to do with Lakeline Corporation, I guess?"

"I can't say—pending ongoing litigation."

"Come on!" I shouted.

"Hey, I'm a corporate officer, there are rules."

"Frank Reynolds," I said as coldly as I could manage. She took a moment to compose her response, wandering past me into the dinning room to take a seat.

"As far as I know, Frank Reynolds is still alive," she said playing randomly with the photographs, papers and books piled on my table.

"The sub had a six hour battery life, maybe twelve hours worth of oxygen. He's been missing for eighteen months!"

"I understand this is hard for you," she said, "But missing is not dead."

"Then where is he?" I said, sweeping everything off the table onto the floor to confront her directly.

"I could ask you the same. You were the last person to see him. We found no body and no submarine. You said he was looking for a passage through the caves to the Sandusky River or Lake Erie. We do not believe such a way out exists."

"You could have waited to install the new safety net. We could have sent another sub or teams of scuba divers."

"We told you both when we were installing it and why. He decided to go and you decided to stay—why is that?"

"Because I'm not a hero." I said, losing impetus to attack her further.

"Exactly, you're not a great liar either," she said, scooping up the mess on the floor and plopping it back on the table. "For instance, you recently told me you gave all this stuff to NASA."

"I gave all my salt mine research to NASA. This is what

I recorded at the Blue Hole, which you already control. If it proves relevant, I'll turn it over also."

"Including this garbage?" she said, picking out two tattered paperbacks of H. P. Lovecraft stories.

"I, I, thought they had some interesting, umm . . . similarities."

"To what, real life?" she scoffed. "These are fiction Sam, a madman's fantasies. You know the old saying about a million monkeys with typewriters producing the works of Shakespeare? This idiot was worth a hundred million monkeys all by himself."

"He describes a creature like we found in the mine," I pleaded. "And carvings of circles, dots and spirals like we saw on, what . . . its prison? And here they are again, underneath each burial niche in the Blue Hole." I showed her drawings of the mine markings and compared them with niche photographs.

"And what, pray tell, does any of these scribbles actually say?"

"Well," I stalled. "I can't be absolutely sure, because . . ."

"Go ahead Professor, take a stab at it."

"Well, this . . . ah phrase here, repeated all around the rim of the . . . ah container, might mean . . . Danger do not open?"

"Ha! Ha! Ha!" she guffawed. "Not even close! But still funny." I slumped back into a chair in defeat. She made a sad, pouty face before trying to console me.

"It's okay Sam, it was mean of me to laugh. Let's start again. This guy Lovecraft," she said, picking up a book and flipping through the pages. "Spent his whole life around

Providence, Rhode Island. No doubt he heard tall, sea tales from fishermen and sailors he was trying to sleep with. Those guys tend to be lonely, drink heavily and believe in shit like sea serpents and mermaids. Maybe that's where this racist sociopath got his paranoid nonsense."

"Now," she said, throwing both paperbacks over her shoulder. "Let *me* tell you a fantasy. Once upon a time (say 600 million years ago), in a faraway land (like the Arctic circle), there was a happy village of little green men and women. The world was much warmer then and all their competitors had brains no bigger than walnuts."

"One day (actually over a century or two), the planet turned much, much colder. The village and its people were frozen solid, scraped off their land and dragged all across Canada in a mile high glacier. Eventually the poor village was dumped in a gigantic ditch (we now call Lake Erie), and thawed out."

"The few survivors (how long can you be freeze-dried), found themselves in a new world, with new competitors, with big, busy brains and fire, tools and weapons who loved to *divide and conquer.* They divided into families, races, religions, tribes, nations and empires just to conquer the living shit out of each other—constantly."

"So this village called Vaarg, hid themselves underwater. Every day since (six thousand years and counting), they sought ways to adapt to their angry new world."

"Wow," I said, coming out of a trance-like focus on Marina's face. *Had her teeth always been so small and pointy?* "That was, umm, amazing? I mean it didn't exactly mesh with anything I've ever found valid, but . . . but . . . Your

MORE GORE FROM CLEVELAND

name is Vaarg, right?"

"BINGO!" she exclaimed. "I am Marina Vaarg. We are all Vaarg. We have always been Vaarg. Even the thing in the freezer at NASA is Vaarg."

"So you belong to some sort of cult?"

"AARRRRGH!" she said. "We're gonna need visual aids. Do you have a magnifying glass of some sort?"

"I should have," I said, getting up to look. "I'm a scientist aren't I?"

"And alcohol, we're also gonna need to drink," she yelled after me.

"White wine good enough?" I said from the kitchen.

"Excellent," she said. "Bring the whole bottle." I found my magnifiers, (two large drink glasses with thick bottoms), that did the same thing. Coming back, she had spread my photos of the Blue Hole mausoleum back on the table.

"Hit me," she said grabbing one glass, and I poured two deep ones and settled down for her lecture contemplating small, pert breasts visible through the spaghetti straps as she leaned over the table. "Now, if you were an ancient race that needed to fit in on a modern planet. . . how would you do it?"

"Learn to shape-shift."

"This isn't the Marvel Universe, Sam—but okay. Think long-term biological."

"Umm . . . evolution?"

"Too long-term, but in the ballpark," she said sucking wine like a parched camel.

"Umm . . . beards, plastic surgery, keto, steroids . . . wait, wait, intermarriage!"

"More likely kidnapping and rape at first but yes, targeted inter-breeding." She slammed her now empty glass atop a figure in the lowest row of the "Native American" burials at the Blue Hole. "Take a gander at him or her—I can't tell from what's left."

"Erie Indians my ass," I growled, examining the shrunken little frog-gnome closely while Marina finished my wine also. "These are humanoids at best."

"You and Frank collected the DNA, and the tests all said—Erie Indian."

"That is ridiculous because nobody knows what Erie DNA looks like because no white man ever saw or tested an Erie Indian dead or alive!."

"You have now, Kemosabe, and wouldn't *any* child of a Native American and . . . *whatever* have at least half Native American DNA?" I grunted reluctant agreement and she told me to look at the third or fourth row—maybe two, three hundred years riper.

"Damn!" I said. "There is a change. They are taller, smaller heads, closer eye sockets." I moved my glass up to examine the upper rows near where we found Jim ensconced among the ancient dead. "Oh my God, you're right! Standing upright they could almost pass for ancient humans!" Marina refilled our glasses and moved away from the table to stand behind me. I drank and pondered while she explained . . .

"And these are workers, the lower classes, born when males were impregnating female Erie. Born in human wombs and raised ashore. Possibly among those wiped-out by other tribes for being so-called "impure". That's when methods changed, Vaarg maidens are now fertilized by human *donors* so to speak. Hatched from eggs, raised underwater, and somewhat surgically altered if necessary. You should see our upper castes now."

"You have castes?" I wondered. "Rigid, from birth classes like Hindus?"

"No, adopted and raised by sacred societies. Dedicated to certain Old Gods, trained, anointed, bled in the name of Cthulhu—then hocus-pocus and POOF—I'm head of Human Resources and Removal. If you want to see an elite, just turn around."

I did, and there stood Marina, gloriously naked, wine in hand, posed like a Burning-Man Festival, Venus-on-the-half-shell, except for the hairy bear-claw slippers she still wore.

"You like?" she said. "Look Sam, I'm sorry to rush things, but it's Mating Season. I'm currently carrying three semi-fresh eggs that need man sauce ASAP. Normally, I'd just go to a bar, hang around the jukebox and take what I could get."

"Every Month?" I gasped, drinking quickly to catch up.

"No, we are not *laying hens*. We mate every ten years. Three eggs, all at once, take it or leave it. I thought it would be nice to choose for a change, someone older and wiser, someone I knew and sort of liked. Are you game for a little interspecies hanky-panky Dr. Samuel Stern?"

"Hell yeah, I feel honored, and I don't have any condoms here anyway. It's been a while for me—a long while actually. I hope you'll be satisfied."

"Let me worry about that—*I'm not a newbie.*"

"Should we go to the bedroom? I can hustle up some clean sheets."

"Do you have a bathtub? Warm water works better for me." Then she took off her slippers and sashayed toward the bathroom on long, delicate, webbed feet.

* * *

The next morning she was gone. I woke up freezing in cold bathwater feeling drugged. My lips were numb from the taste of her blue lipstick. I dried off, wrapped a bathrobe around my shivering body and wandered into the dining room.

Everything was pretty much as we had left it. I took the wine bottle and two glasses and put them in the sink. On the counter were two hand-written letters.

Dear Sam, Thanks for a lovely evening. You were better than expected. I hope you remember most of it. Here's the hard part; We will never meet again unless you attempt to endanger us. If so, take out accident insurance—immediately.

We will never mate again, you will never meet your offspring, but I promise to try enrolling one in your seminar - If you're still teaching, (we mature faster and live much longer than you).

P.S. Kevin & Nora are eager to hear about my "dissertation."
Something Like Love — Marina.

The second letter was a page of carefully drawn, swirling circles, curves, dots, spirals and other markings like I found and failed to translate at the the Salt Mine or the Blue Hole. Nothing I had seen was this extensive or varied. Attached was a sticky note.

Dear Samuel Stern, this Rosetta Stone is for you. It is the Pledge of Allegiance—"I pledge allegiance to the flag of the United States of America - blah, blah, blah." Better get busy Professor, we are all Americans and it's about time we understood each other.

MORE
GORE
from
CLEVELAND

About The Author

Craig A. Webb is and old, hippie-clown with a degree in Theatre and Communications from Cleveland State University. He has performed all across the United States from New York to  California while traveling with two circuses and three Shakespeare companies—but never made it to Alaska or Hawaii. However, most of his life has been spent working as a Traffic Control Supervisor on the roads and highways in and around Cleveland, Ohio. If you've found yourself helplessly marooned in traffic, anywhere in the North East Ohio vicinity, for the last forty years—it was likely because of him.

He has always enjoyed writing, be it plays, stories or angry letters to the editor of his high school newspaper, college newspaper, or The Cleveland Plain Dealer. Let's just say he has many, "unorthodox" opinions. So now, in retirement, it is no surprise he is writing books. This is his third attempt. God willing, it probably won't be his last.

What Is This About?

Basically this is about a kid who grew up liking ghost stories told by his father and others around the campfire on family fishing trips and vacations. Never a fan of "slasher flicks" he gravitated to more intellectual tales of monsters, curses and the always fatal hubris of wayward science and religion. Eventually that "less-traveled" fork in the literary woods leads to H.P. Lovecraft. If you wish to know more about him, God Bless your endangered soul as you read his work. I'd start with The Shadow Over Innsmouth and The Dunwich Horror.

Being so inflicted, I noticed there were very few novels or short stories set in my local haunt of Cleveland. Readers think they know of New York City, Los Angeles, Chicago and other places mostly because lots of books and movies are set there.

Thus, my brand of "local horror" is focused on "The Best Location In The Nation" or "The Mistake On The Lake" depending on ones' opinion of the Cleveland Chamber of Commerce.

So, my first collection of short stories, The Shadow over Cleveland was all about strange, bizarre and terrifying stuff happening locally—including the machinations of a loathsome, ancient race living in Lake Erie. I called them The Vaarg.

Folks in my writing workshops wanted to know all about the Vaarg. How they lived, what they wanted and exactly how they looked—but I don't write travelogues.

In cryptic response, this collection, More Gore From Cleveland is full-up with Vaarg— where they hang out, what they do, even who they screw. You might say this book is a vivid example of the old admonition, "Be careful what you ask for."

Since Early Years
Craig A. Webb

Other Works

by Craig A. Webb —*Now available at Lulu.com*

VAROOM the Passion of E.Z. Cash

Almost nobody knows of the obscure religion that deifies HENRY FORD, founded by its charismatic messenger the Reverend Ernest Zachary Cash. This newly authorized, founding testament corrects this historic anomaly, leaping from the far future to the not so distant past and back again.

As the FORD believed, "let the buyer beware."

THE SHADOW OVER CLEVELAND
13 LoveCrafted Tales.

Craig A. Webb's Thirteen Lovecrafted Tales brings all the mayhem, menace and madness right to your doorstep. Over our parks, neighborhoods, workplaces and institutions the shadow looms.

Sly, wry and clever, these stories peer into the dark corners of Cleveland.

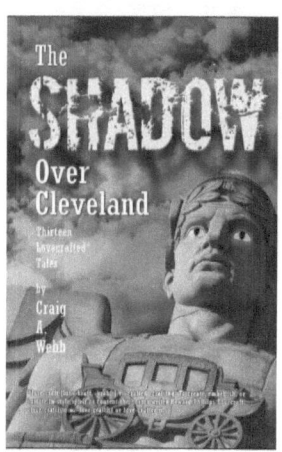

www.ingramcontent.com/pod-product-compliance
Lightning Source LLC
Chambersburg PA
CBHW050422260626
47156CB00003B/1111